For my village —S.L.

For Sina & Tim —M.L.

Text copyright © 2021 by Suzanne Lang
Jacket art and interior illustrations copyright © 2021 by Max Lang

All rights reserved. Published in the United States by Random House Studio, an imprint of
Random House Children's Books, a division of Penguin Random House LLC, New York.

Random House Studio and the colophon are registered trademarks of Penguin Random House LLC.

RH Graphic with the book design is a trademark of Penguin Random House LLC.

GRUMPY MONKEY is a registered trademark of Pick & Flick Pictures, Inc.

Visit us on the Web! rhcbooks.com

Educators and librarians, for a variety of teaching tools, visit us at RHTeachersLibrarians.com

Library of Congress Cataloging-in-Publication Data is available upon request.
ISBN 978-0-593-30601-7 (trade) — ISBN 978-0-593-30602-4 (lib. bdg.) —
ISBN 978-0-593-30603-1 (ebook)
MANUFACTURED IN CHINA
10 9 8 7 6 5 4 3 2
First Edition

GRUMPY MONKEY
FRESHLY SQUEEZED

By Suzanne Lang

Illustrated by Max Lang

RANDOM HOUSE STUDIO  **NEW YORK**

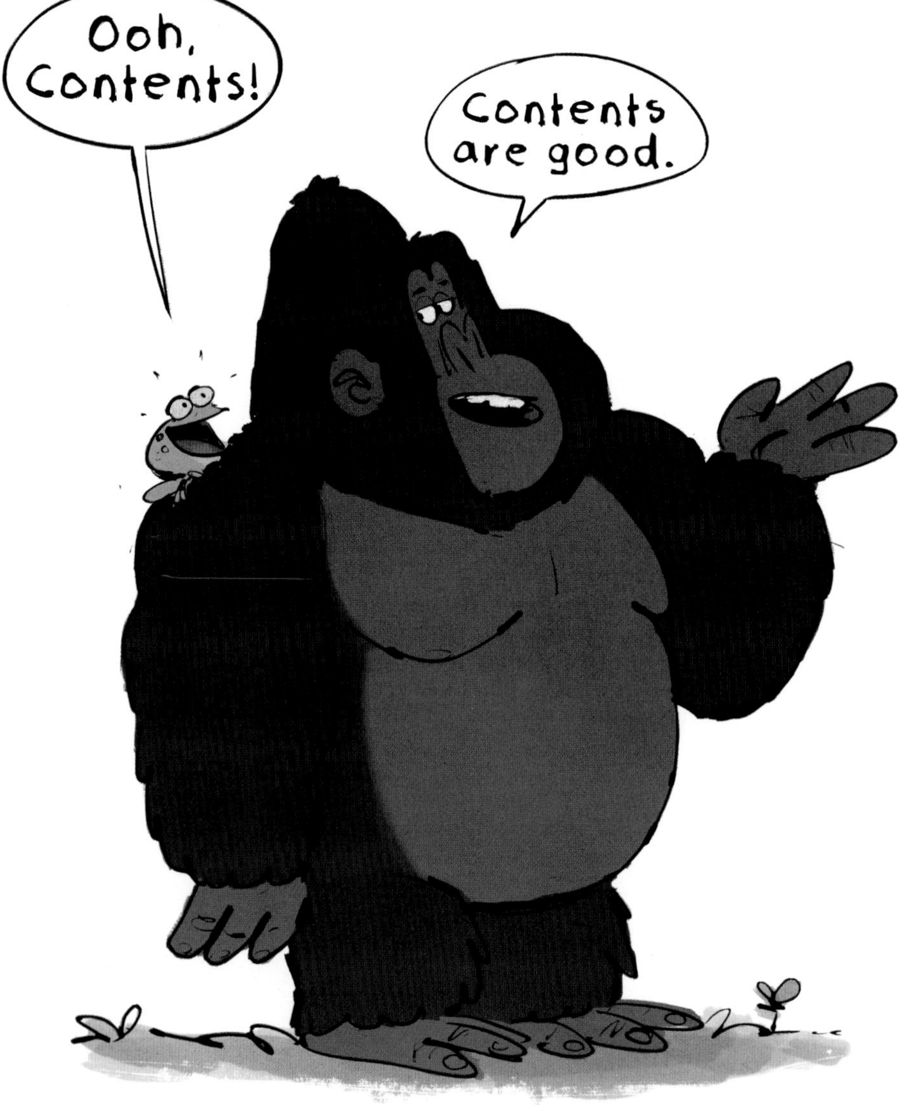
Ooh, Contents!
Contents are good.

CONTENTS

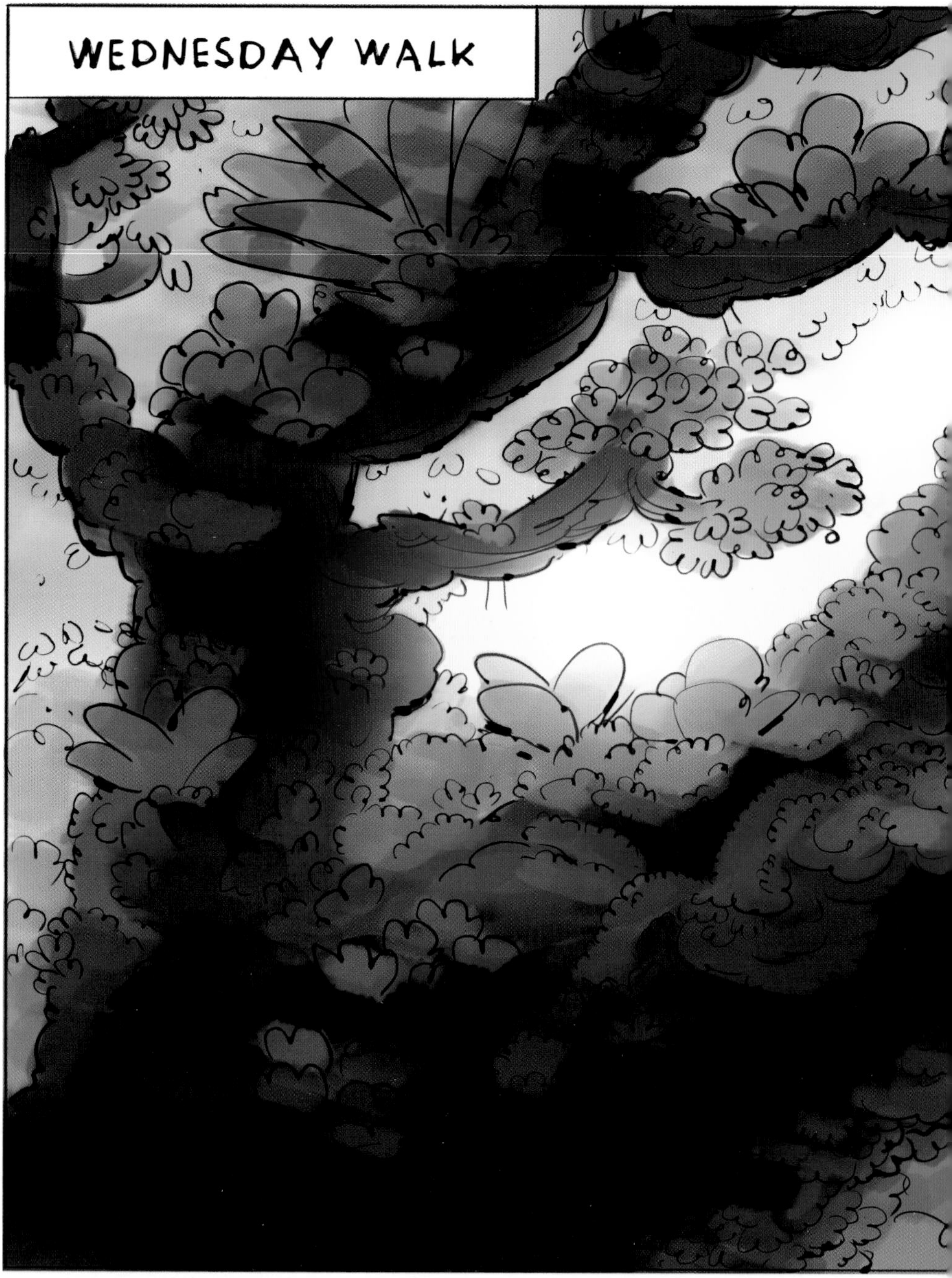
WEDNESDAY WALK

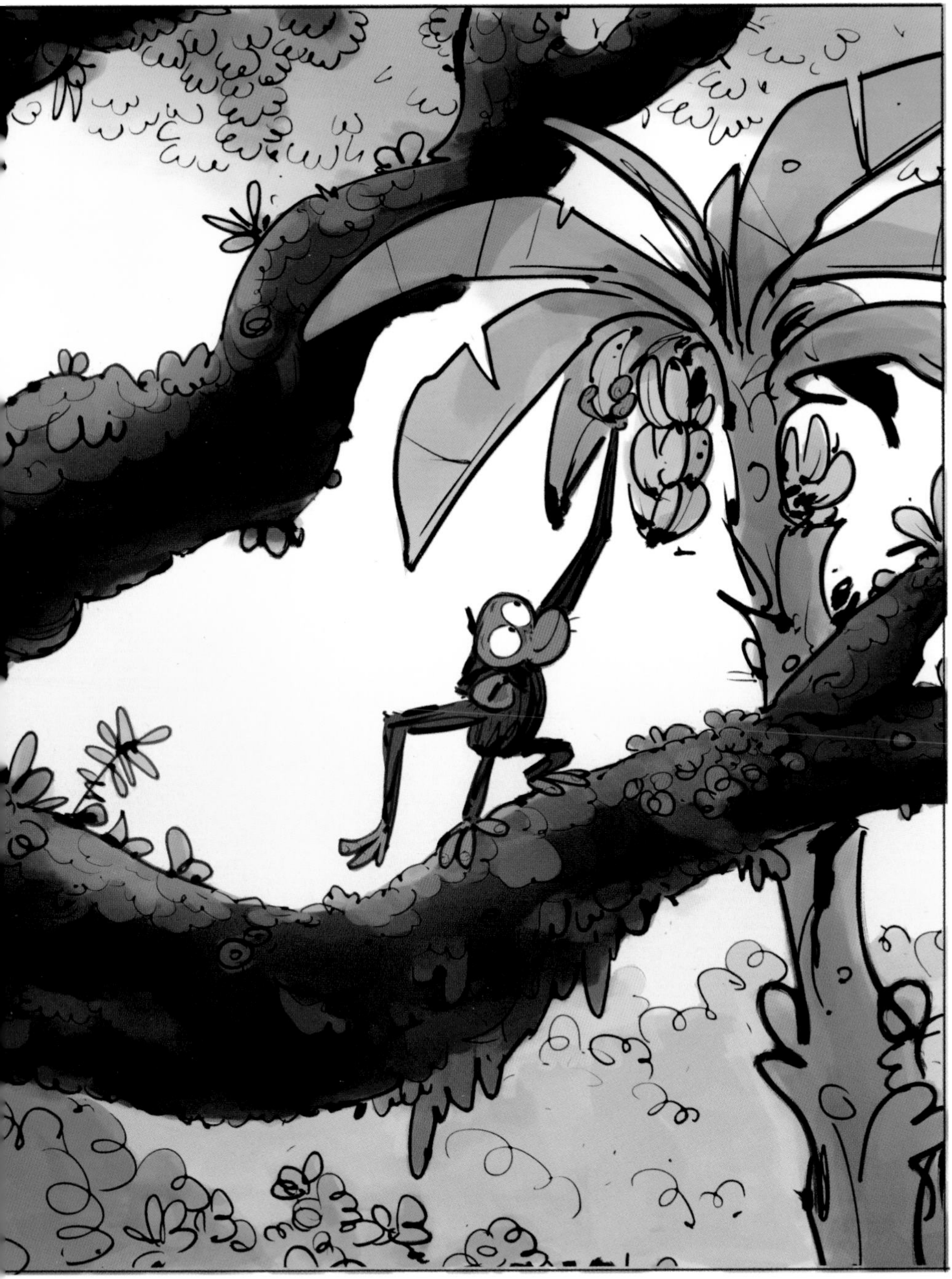

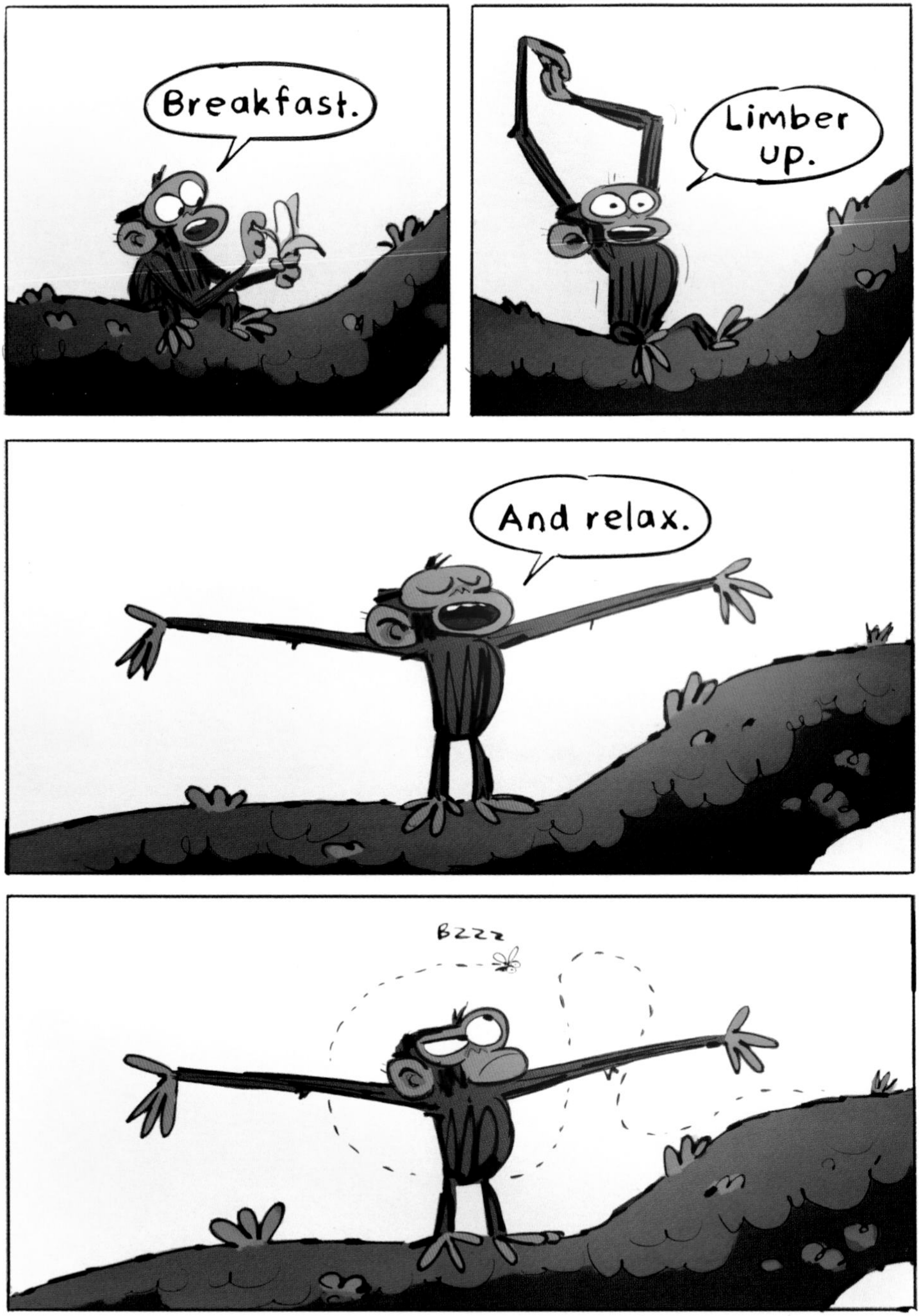
Breakfast.
Limber up.
And relax.
Bzzz

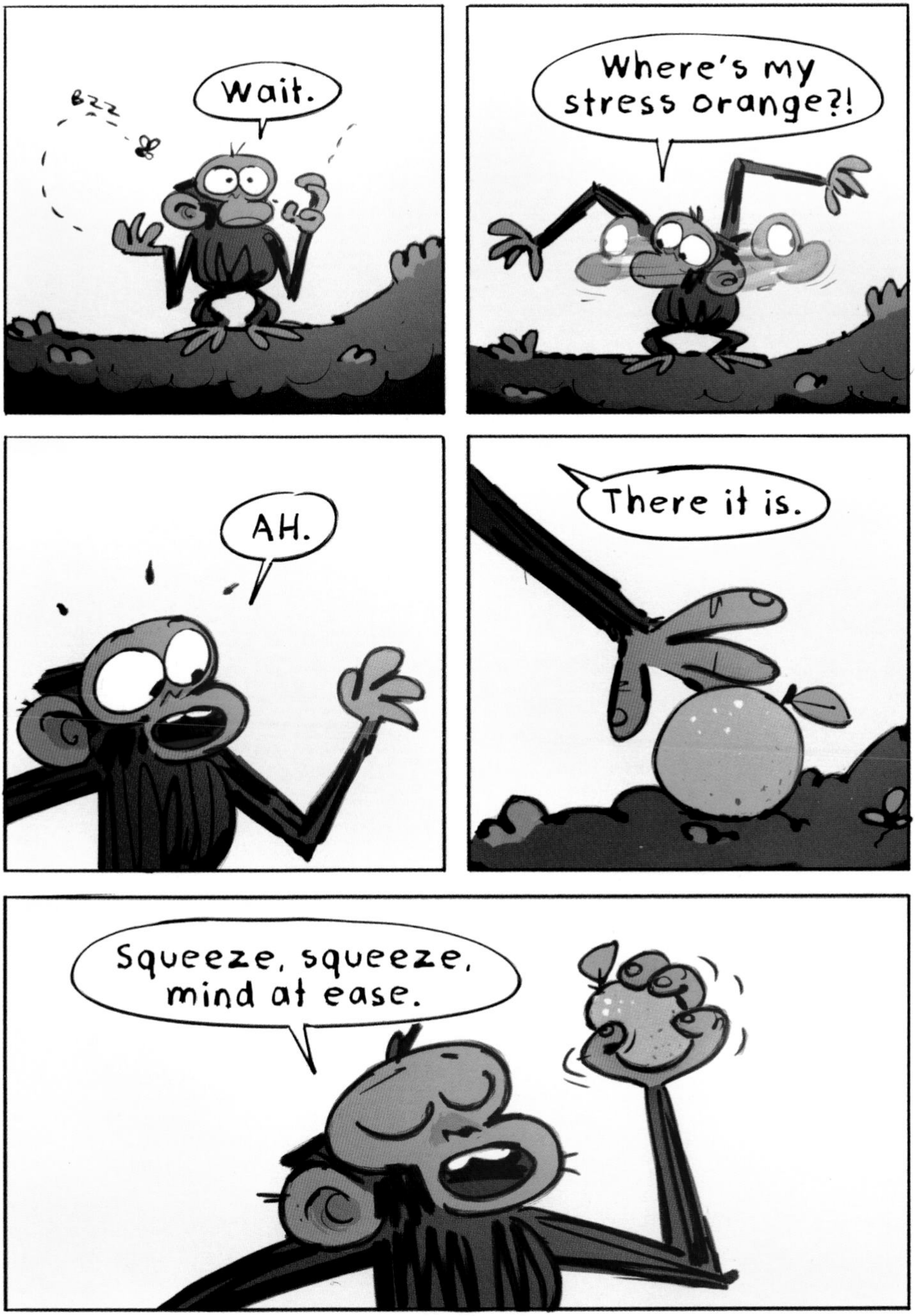
BZZ
Wait.
Where's my stress orange?!
AH.
There it is.
Squeeze, squeeze, mind at ease.

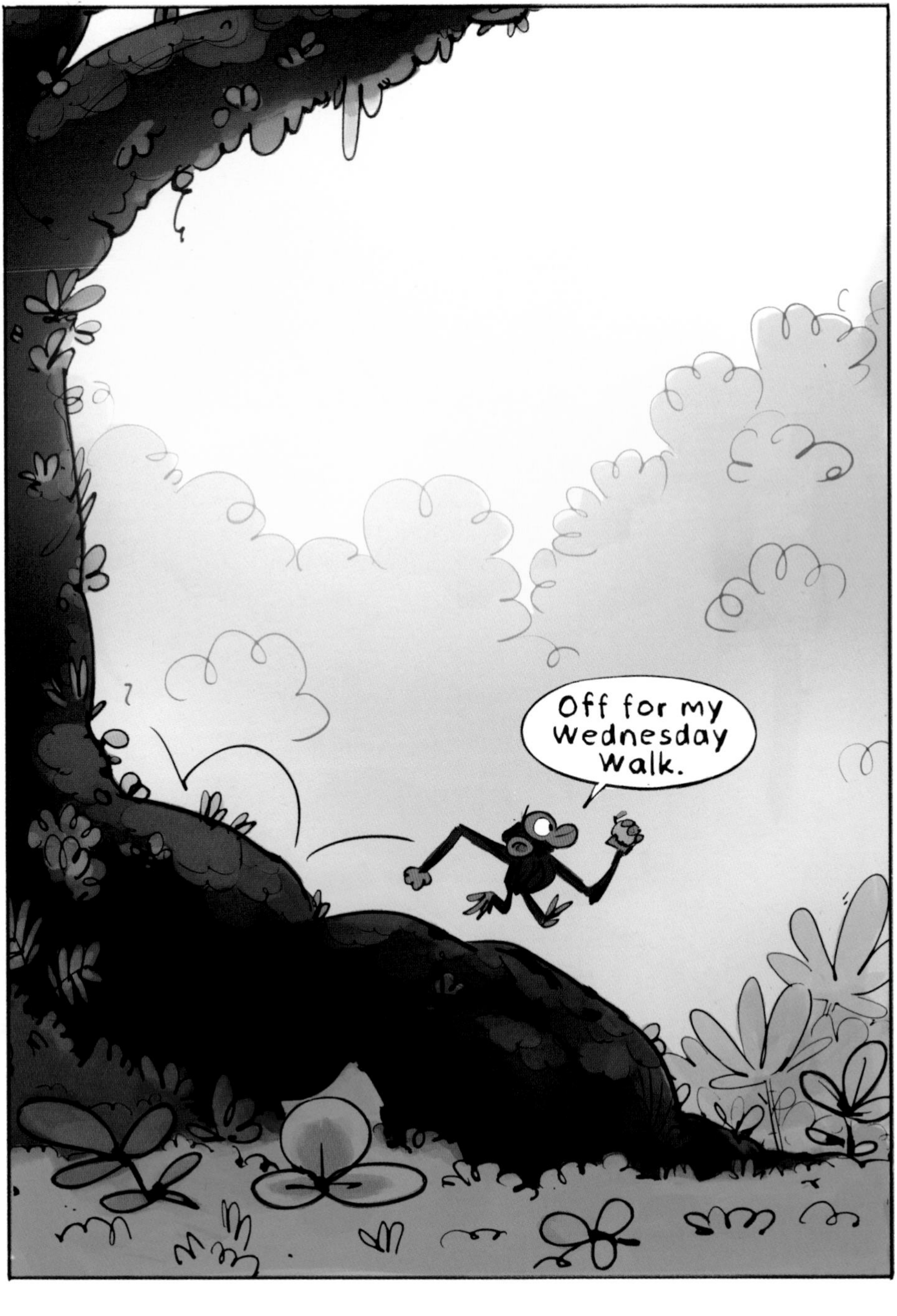
Off for my Wednesday walk.

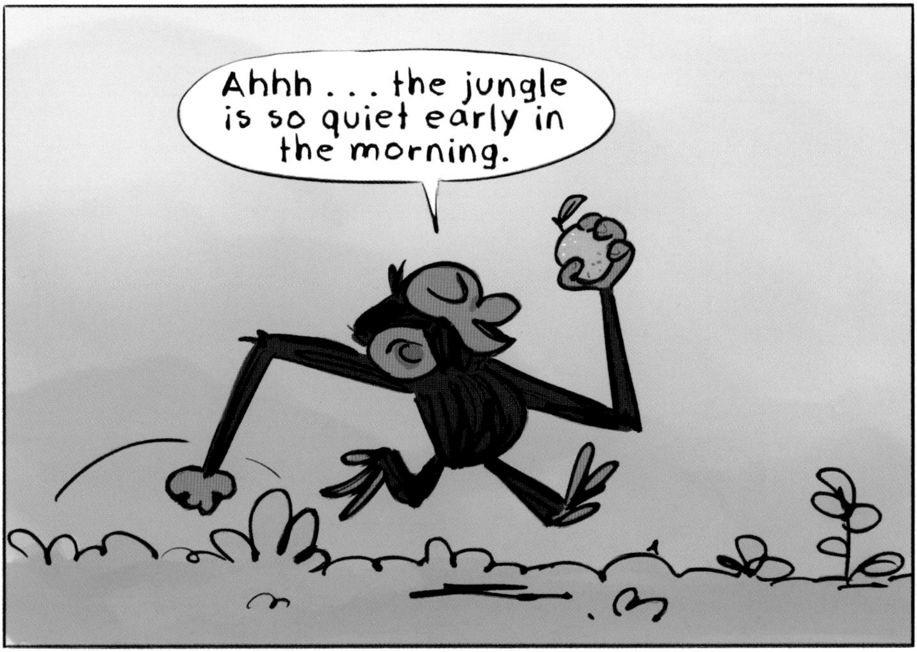
Ahhh . . . the jungle is so quiet early in the morning.

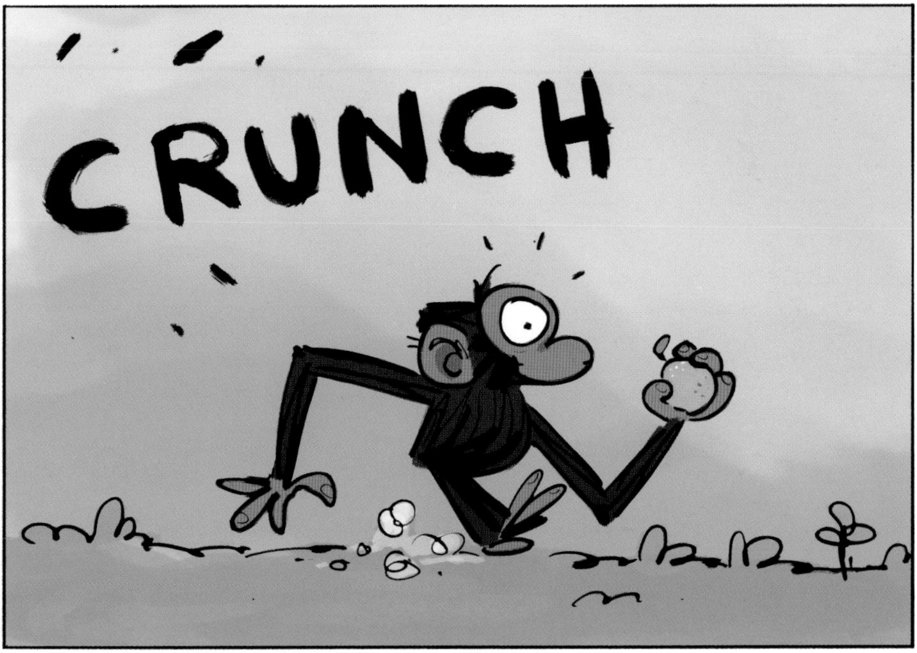
CRUNCH

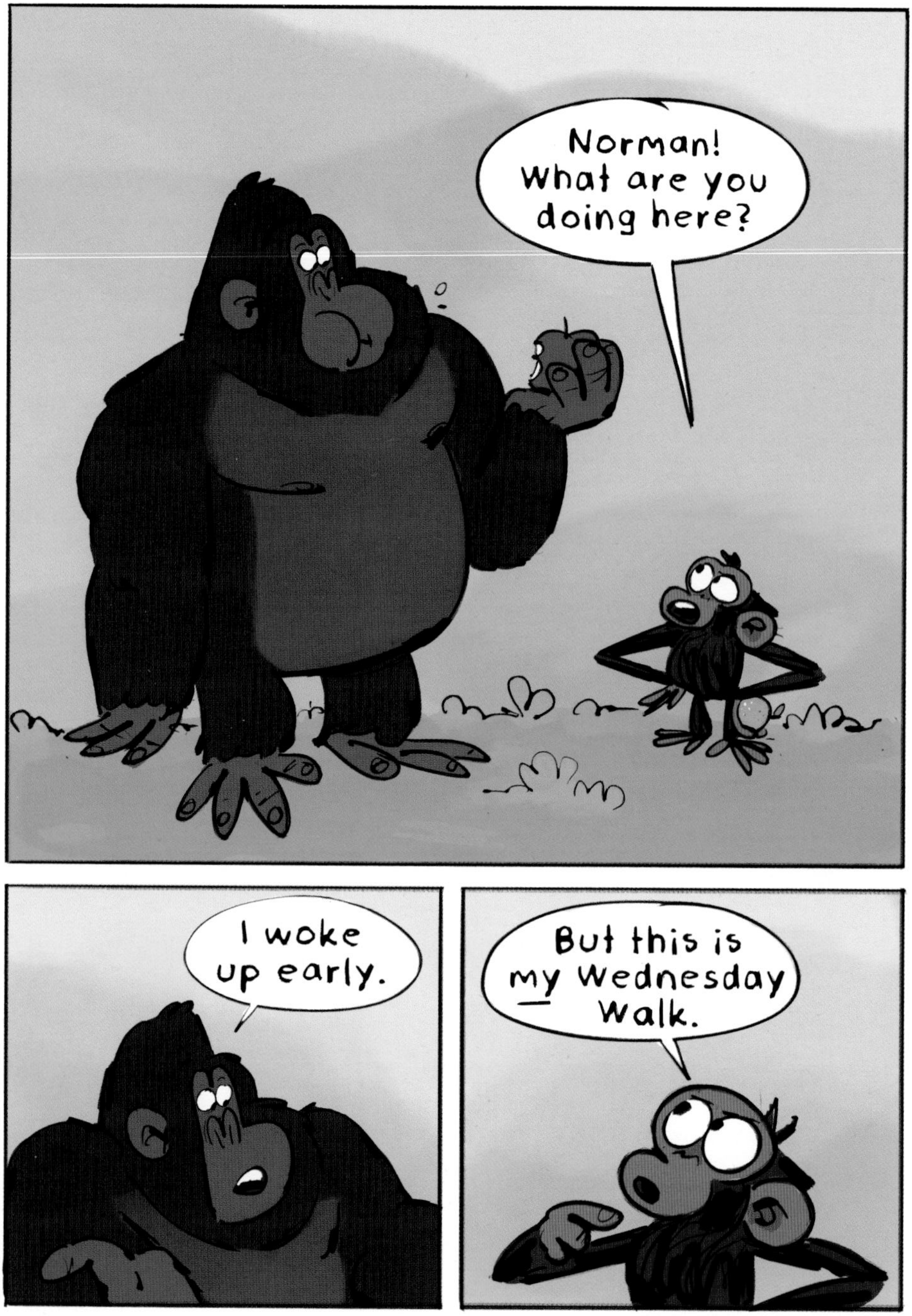
Norman! What are you doing here?
I woke up early.
But this is my Wednesday Walk.

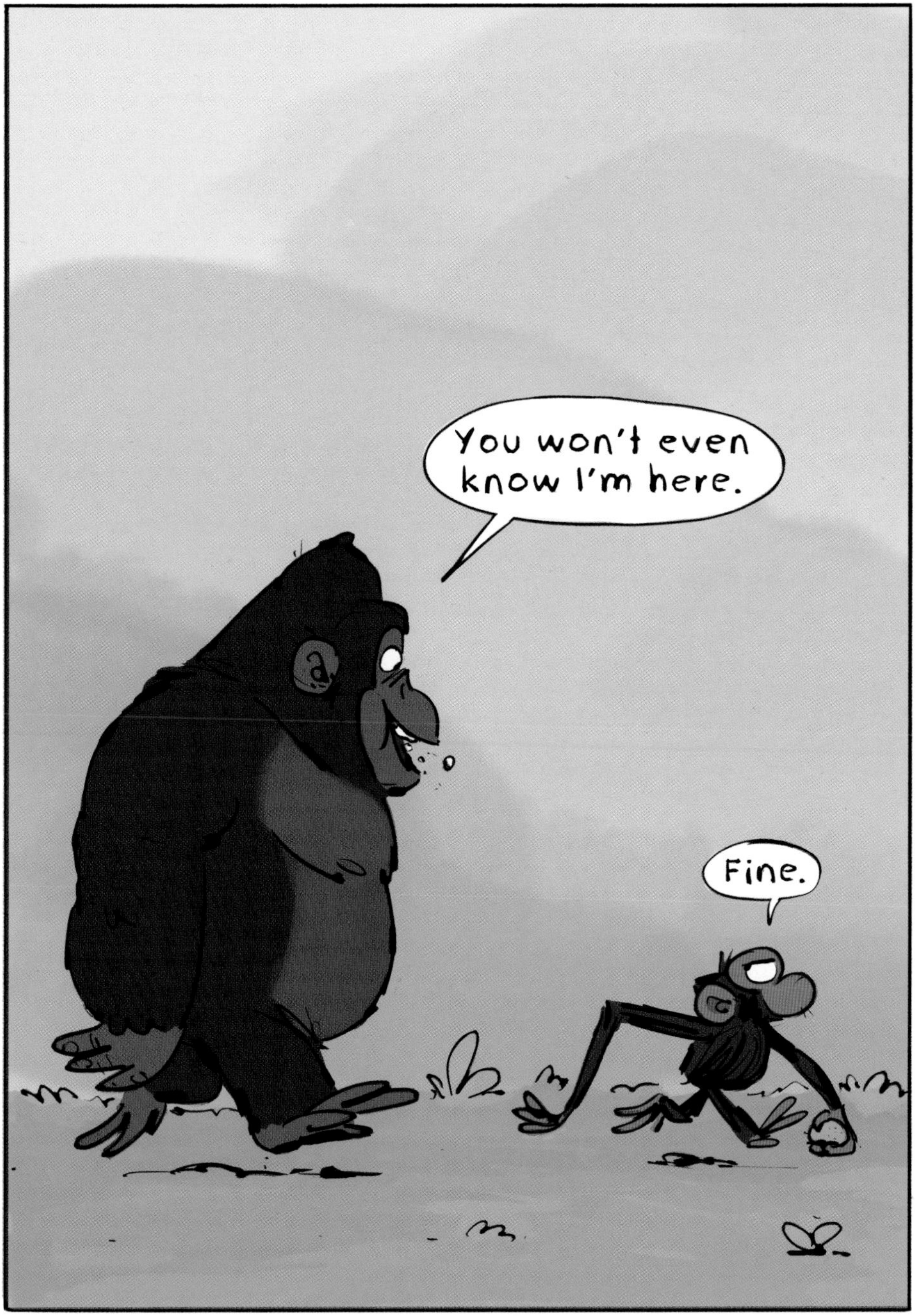
You won't even know I'm here.
Fine.

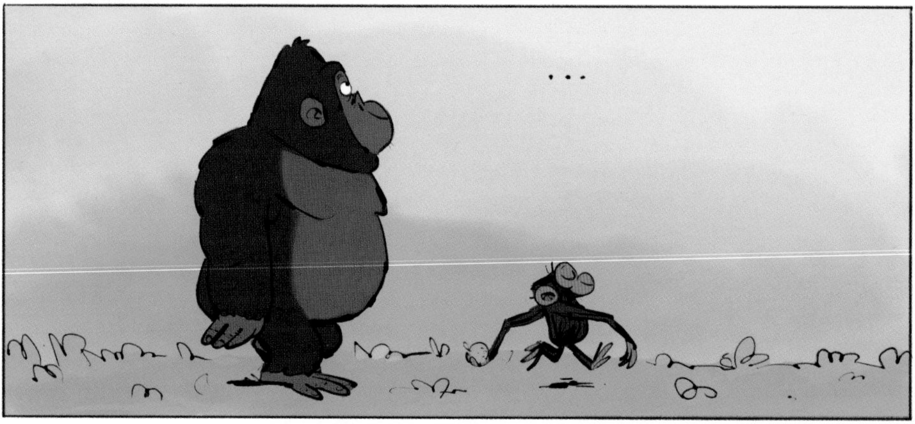
...

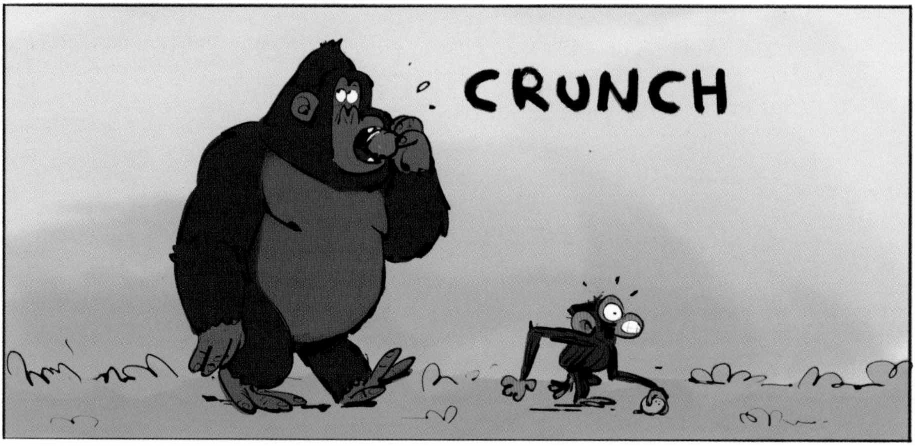
CRUNCH

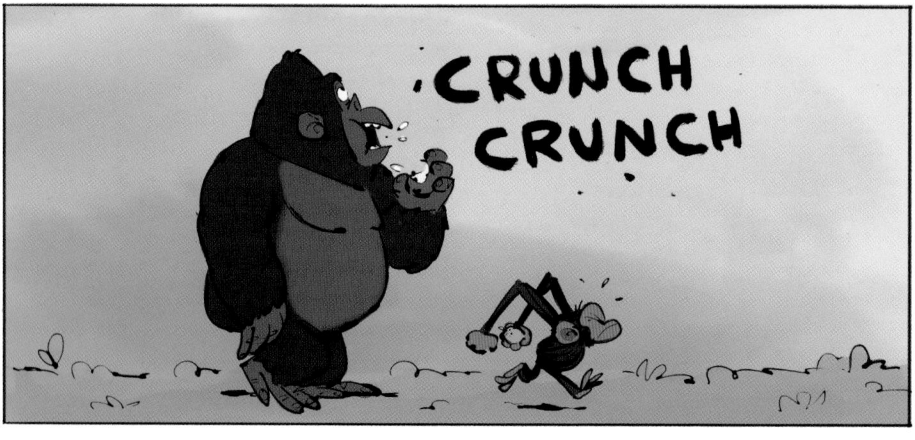
CRUNCH
CRUNCH

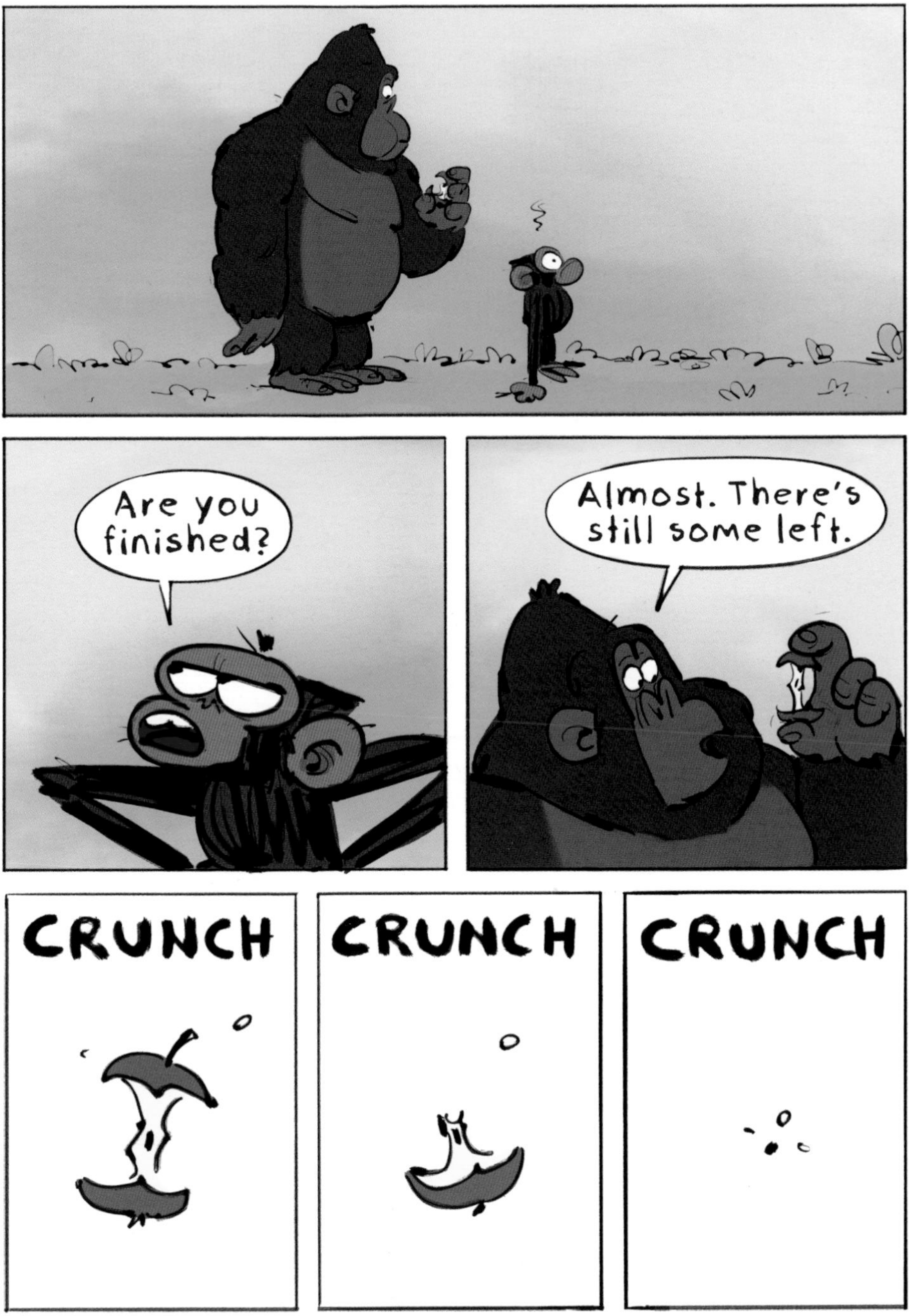
Are you finished?
Almost. There's still some left.
CRUNCH
CRUNCH
CRUNCH

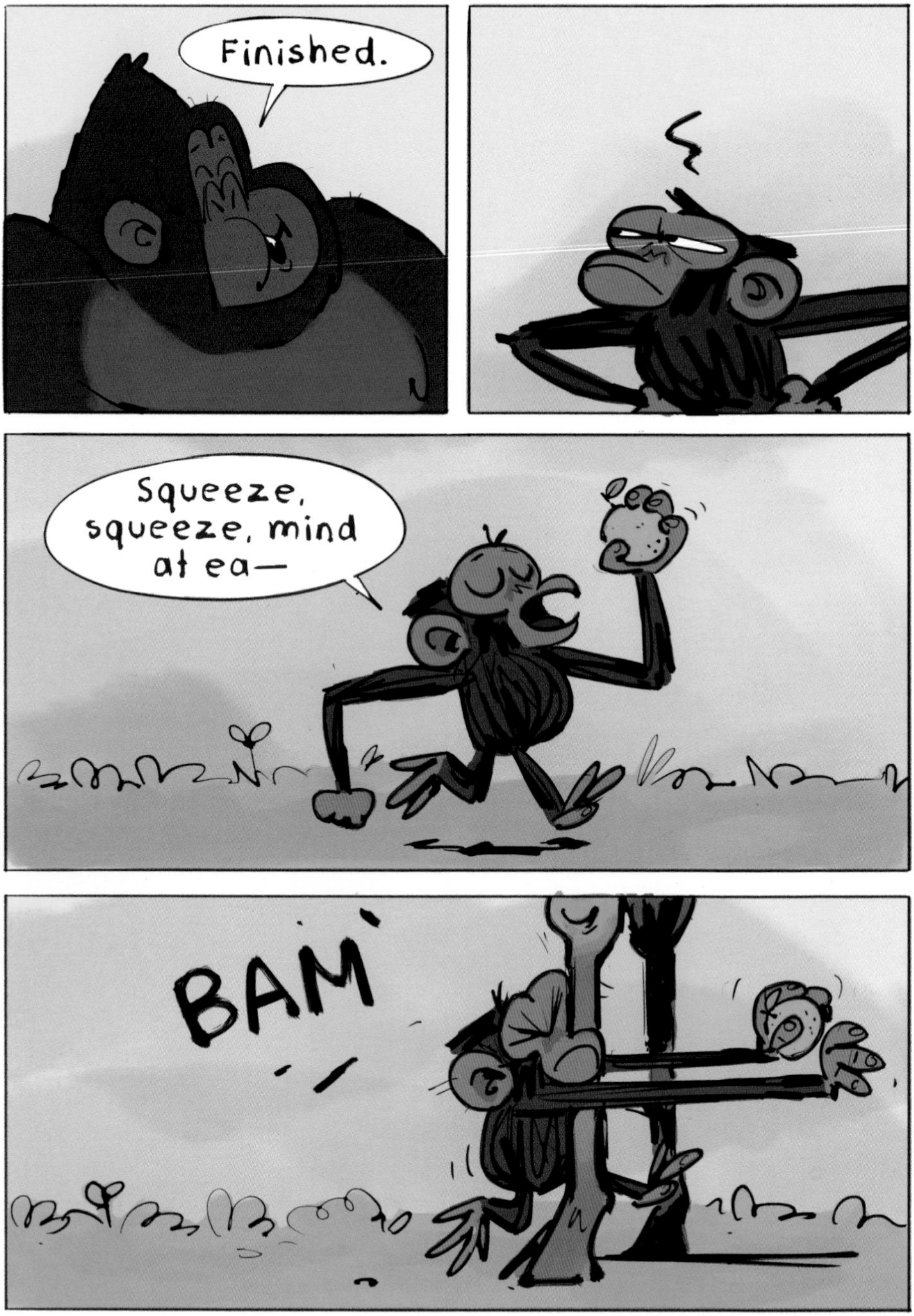
Finished.
Squeeze, squeeze, mind at ea—
BAM

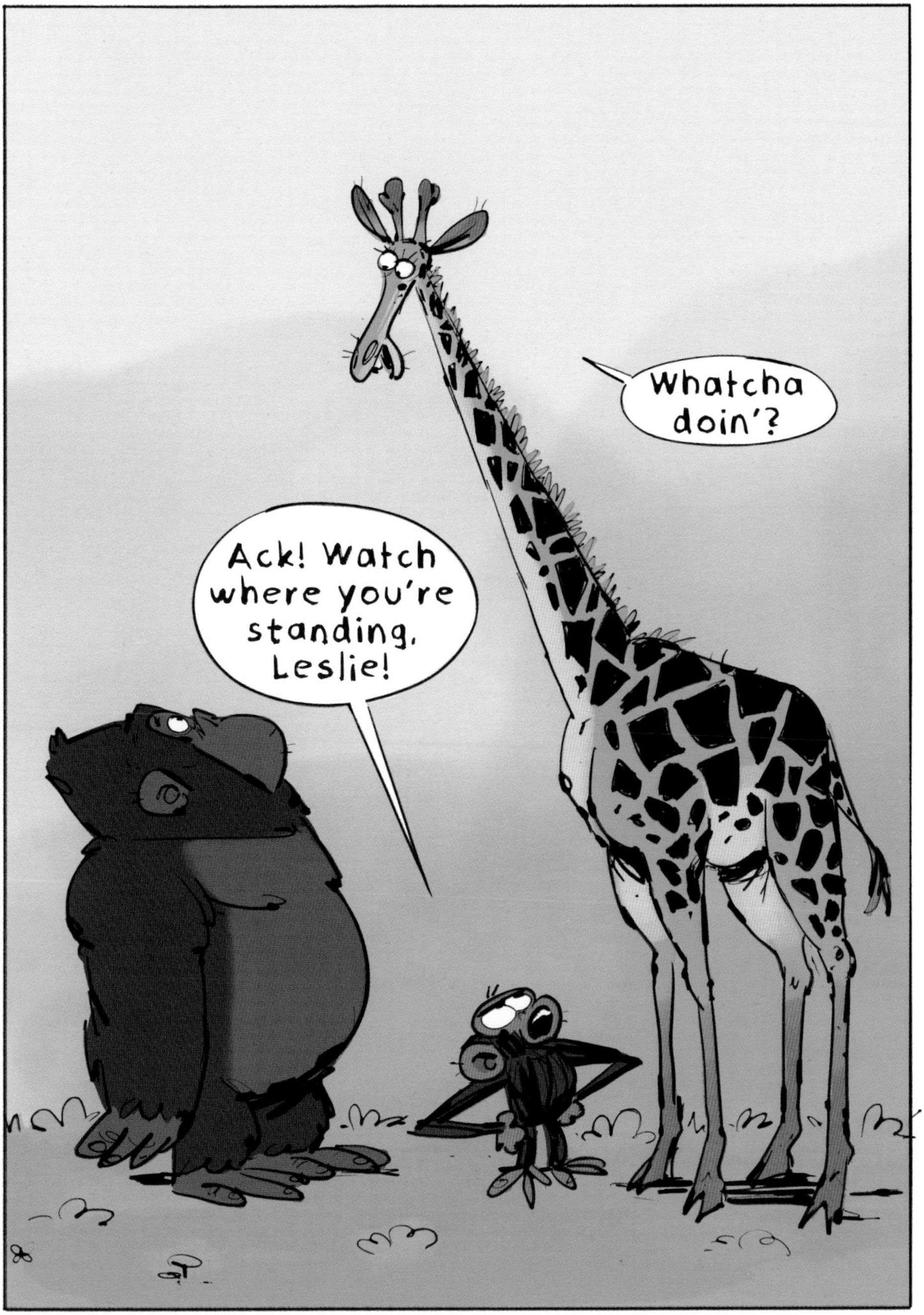
Whatcha doin'?
Ack! Watch where you're standing, Leslie!

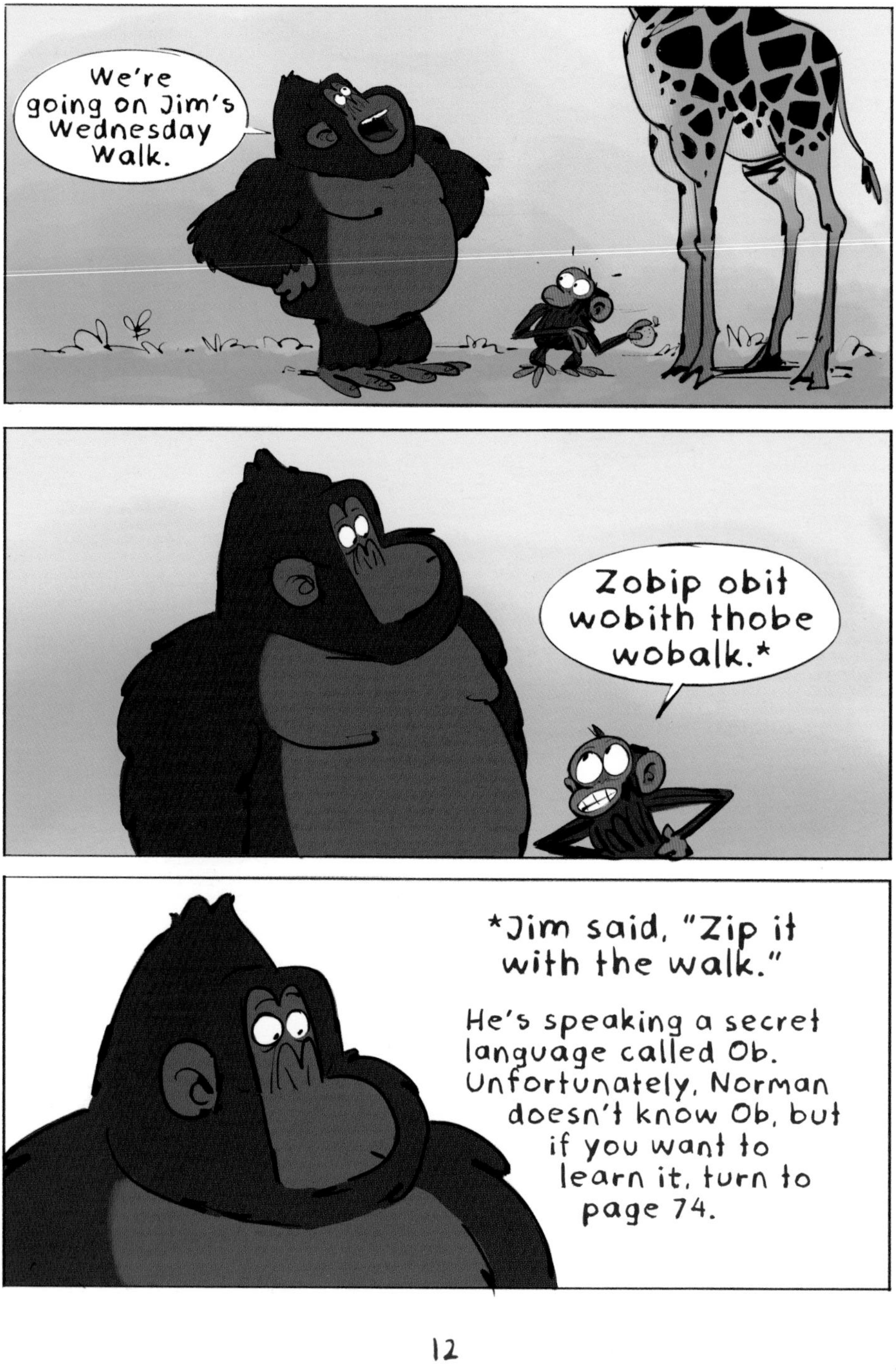
We're going on Jim's Wednesday Walk.
Zobip obit wobith thobe wobalk.*
*Jim said, "Zip it with the walk."
He's speaking a secret language called Ob. Unfortunately, Norman doesn't know Ob, but if you want to learn it, turn to page 74.

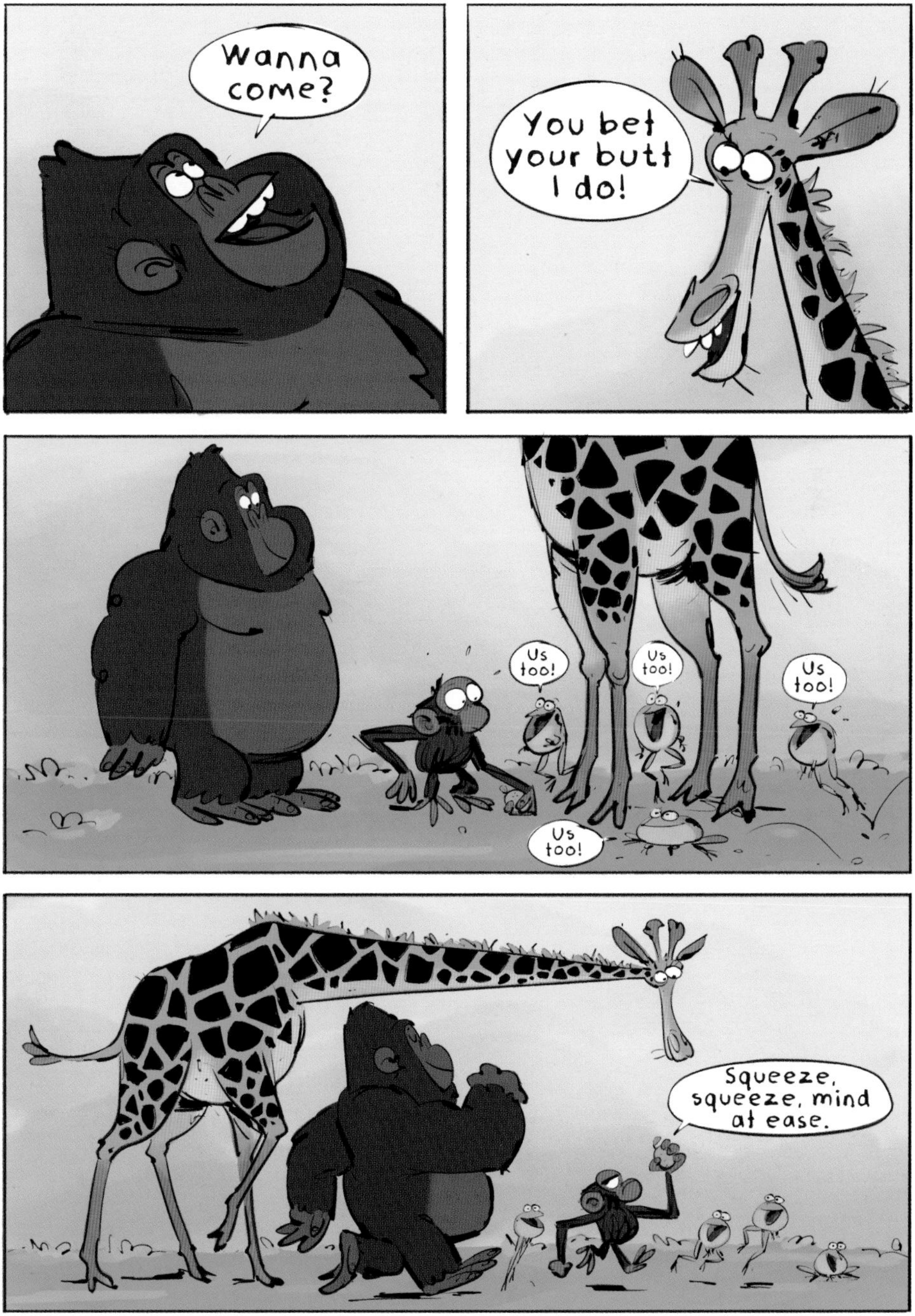
Wanna come?
You bet your butt I do!
Us too!
Us too!
Us too!
Us too!
Squeeze, squeeze, mind at ease.

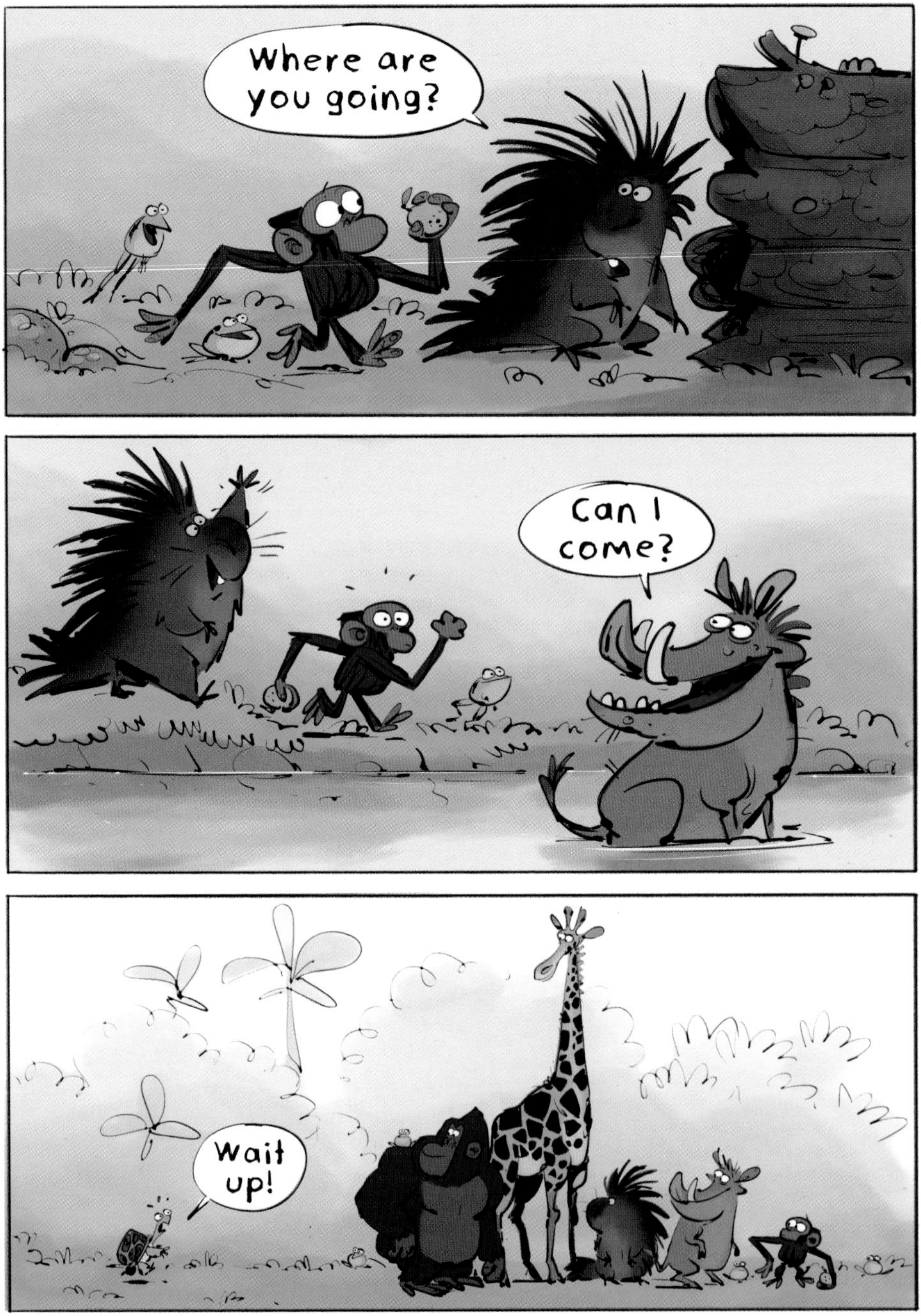
Where are you going?
Can I come?
Wait up!

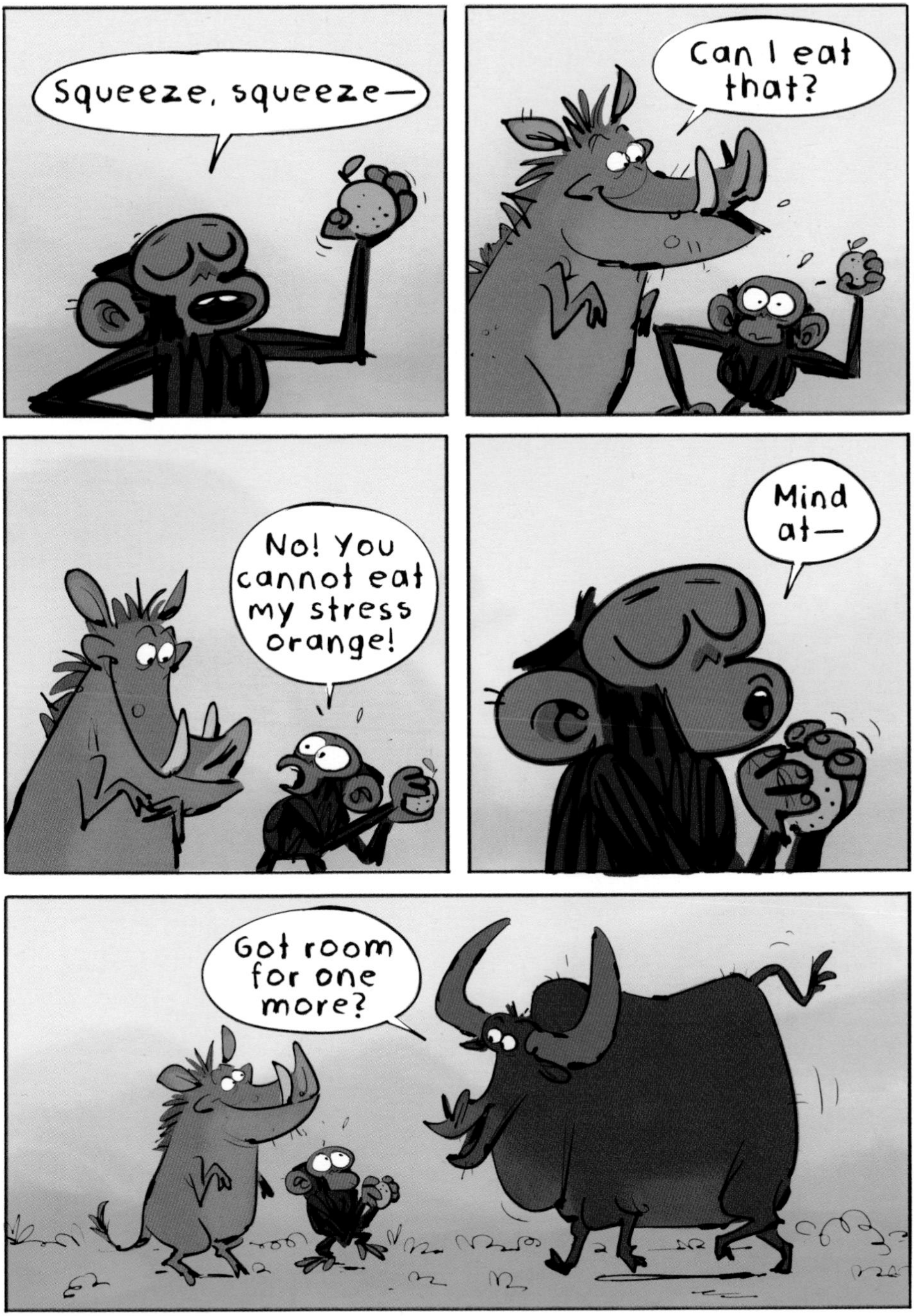
Squeeze, squeeze—
Can I eat that?
No! You cannot eat my stress orange!
Mind at—
Got room for one more?

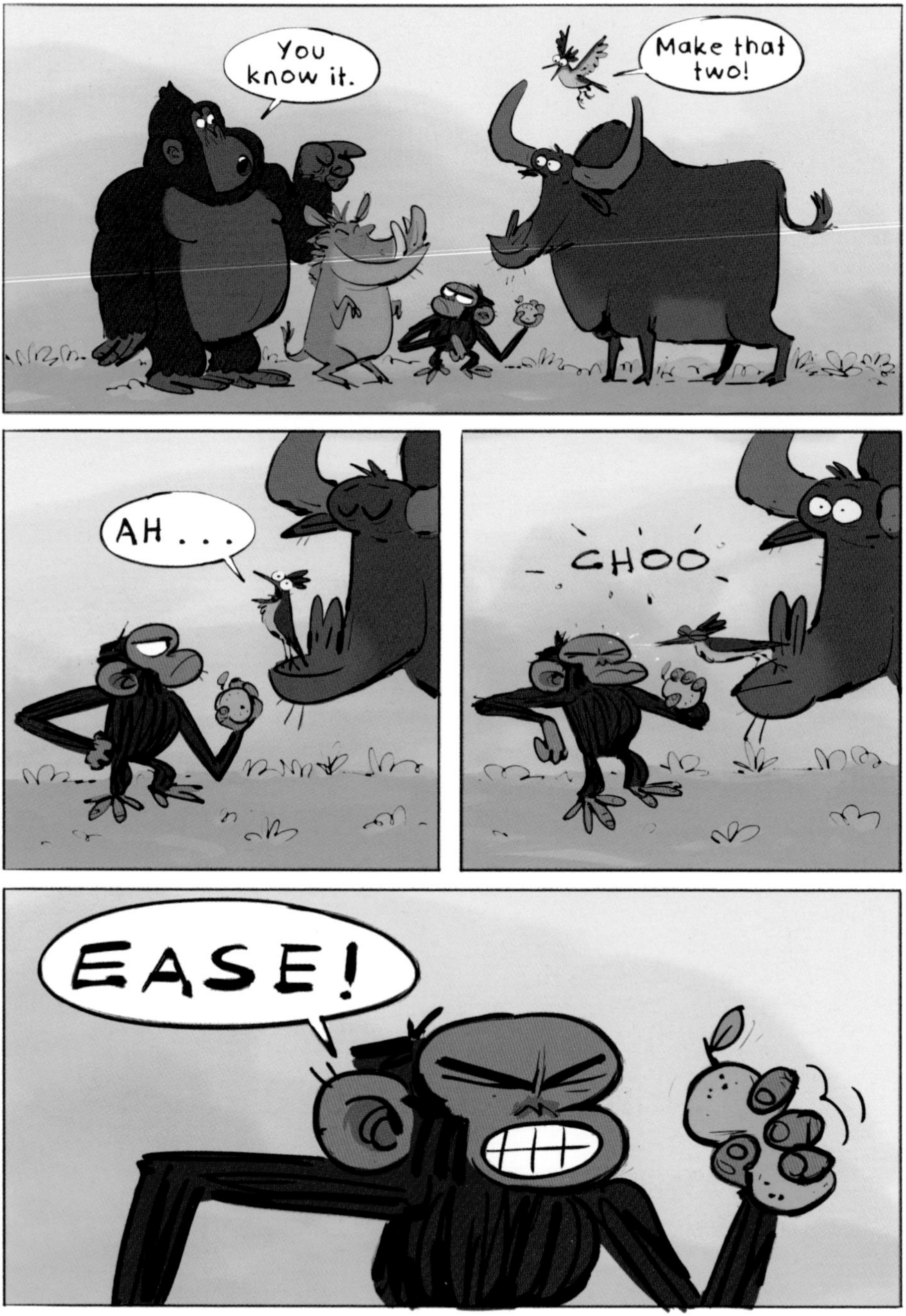
You know it.
Make that two!
AH . . .
CHOO
EASE!

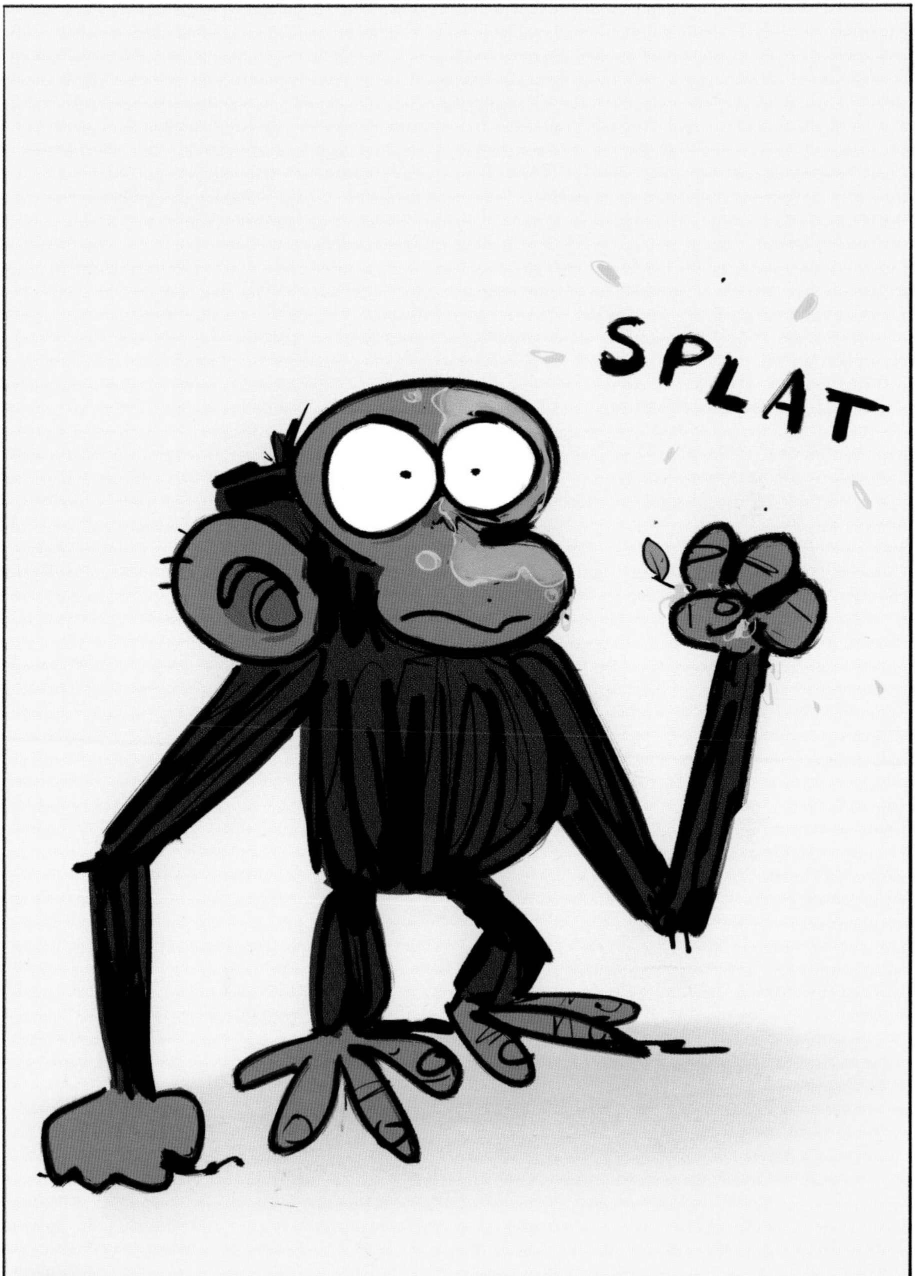
SPLAT

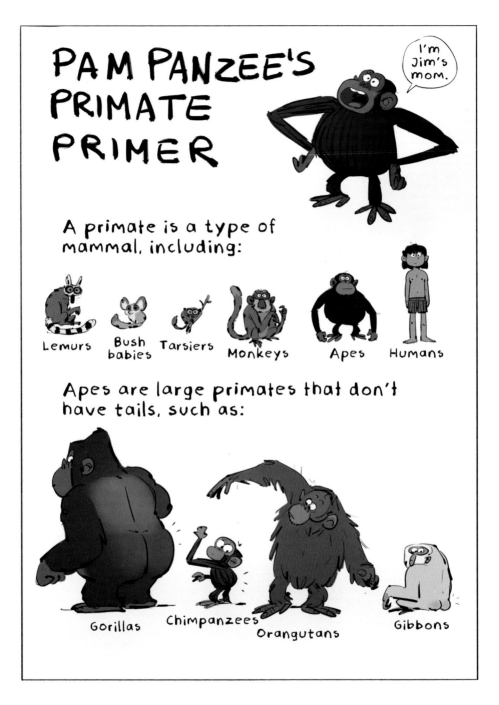

PAM PANZEE'S PRIMATE PRIMER

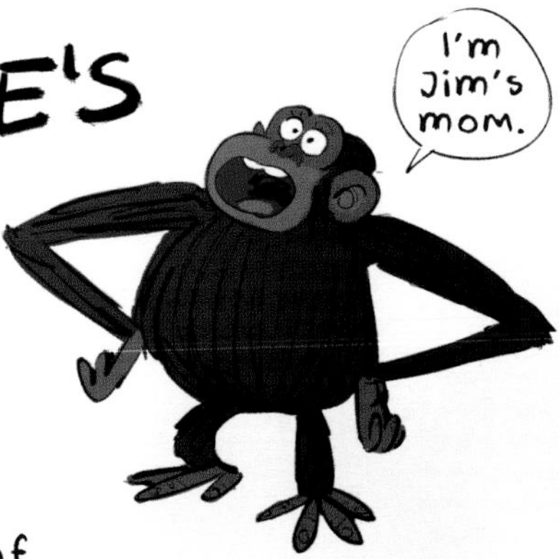
I'm Jim's mom.

A primate is a type of mammal, including:

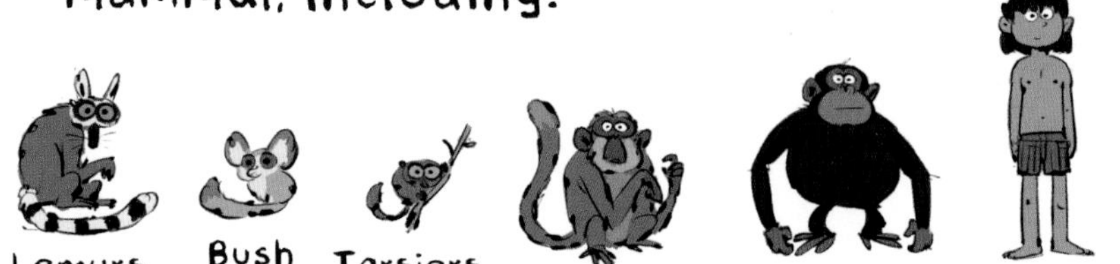
Lemurs
Bush babies
Tarsiers
Monkeys
Apes
Humans

Apes are large primates that don't have tails, such as:

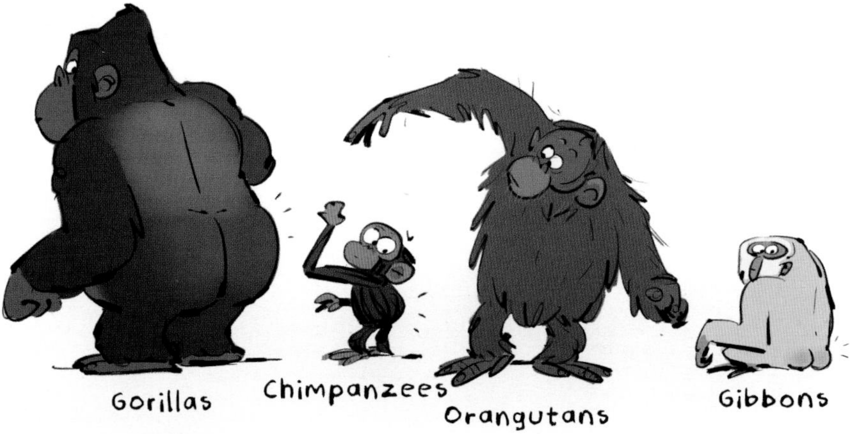
Gorillas
Chimpanzees
Orangutans
Gibbons

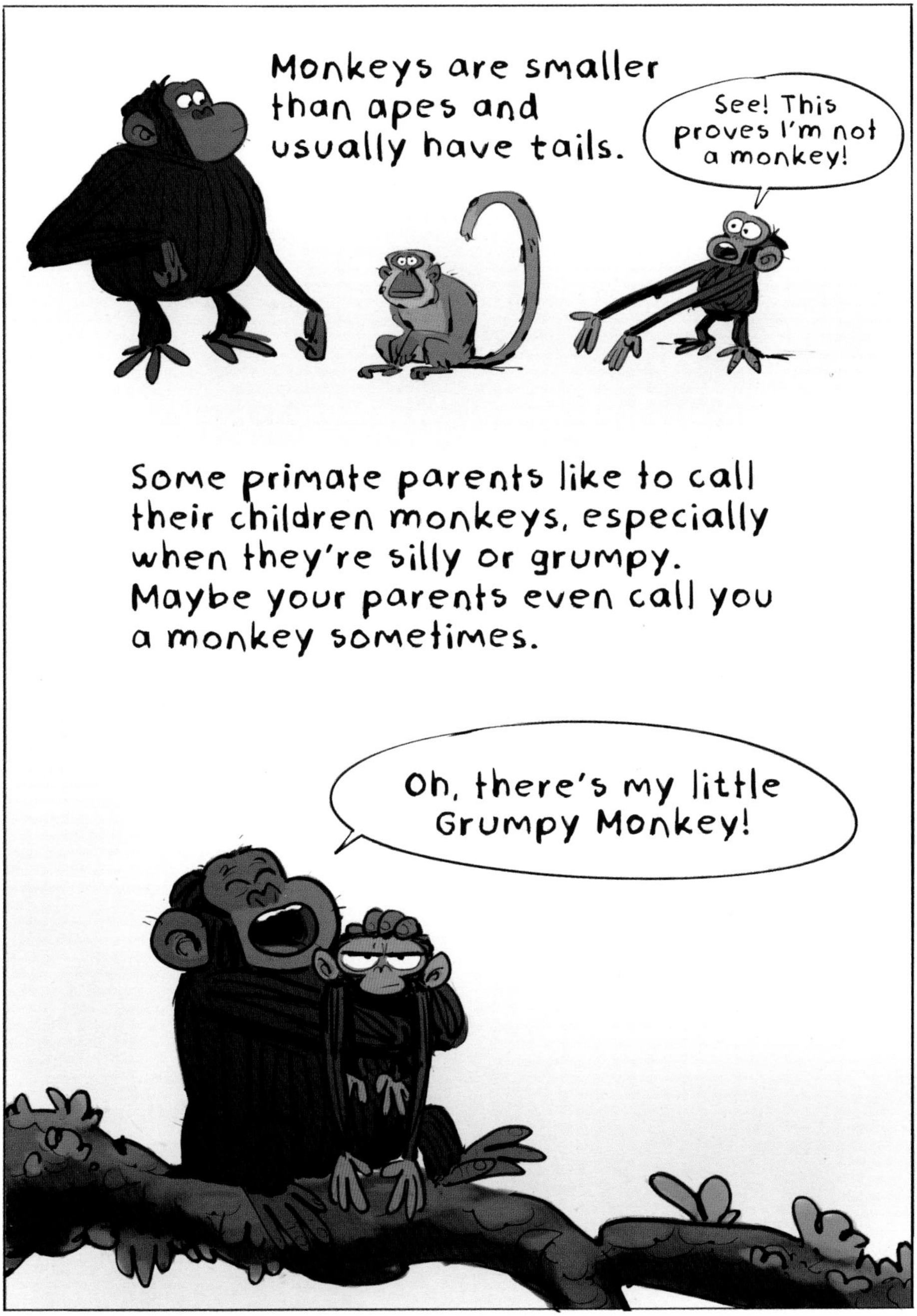
Monkeys are smaller than apes and usually have tails.
See! This proves I'm not a monkey!
Some primate parents like to call their children monkeys, especially when they're silly or grumpy. Maybe your parents even call you a monkey sometimes.
Oh, there's my little Grumpy Monkey!

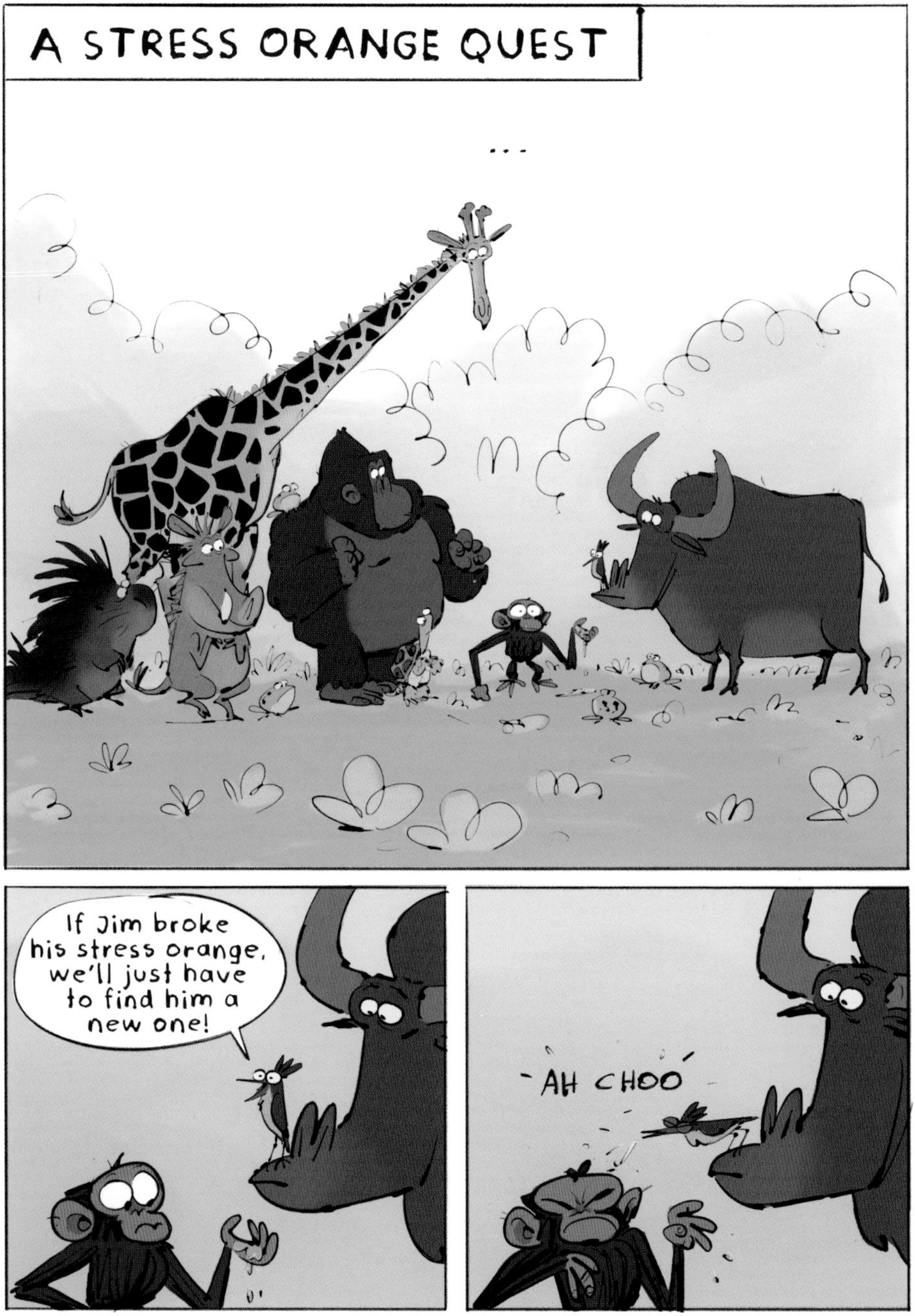
A STRESS ORANGE QUEST
...
If Jim broke his stress orange, we'll just have to find him a new one!
AH CHOO

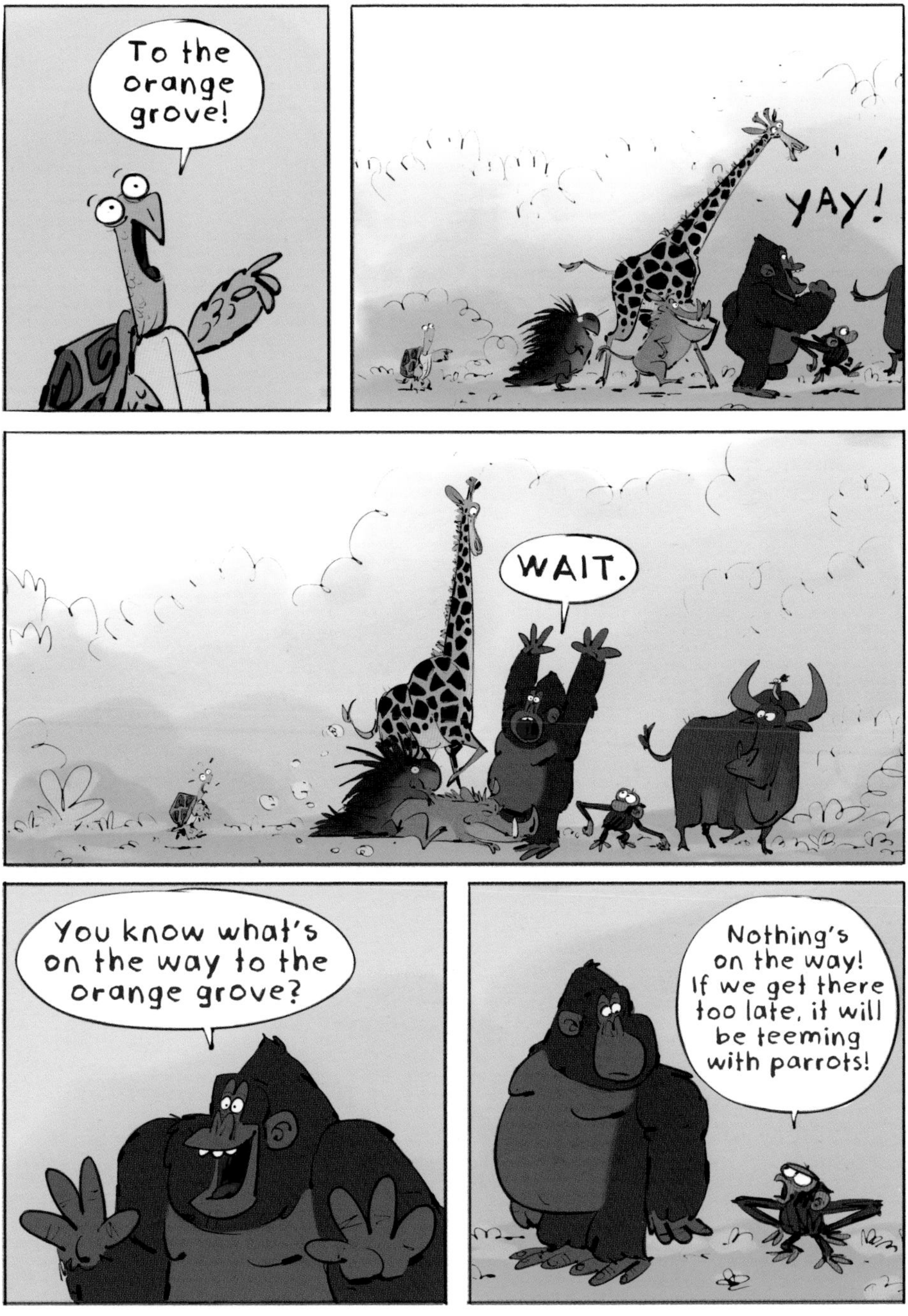
To the orange grove!
YAY!
WAIT.
You know what's on the way to the orange grove?
Nothing's on the way! If we get there too late, it will be teeming with parrots!

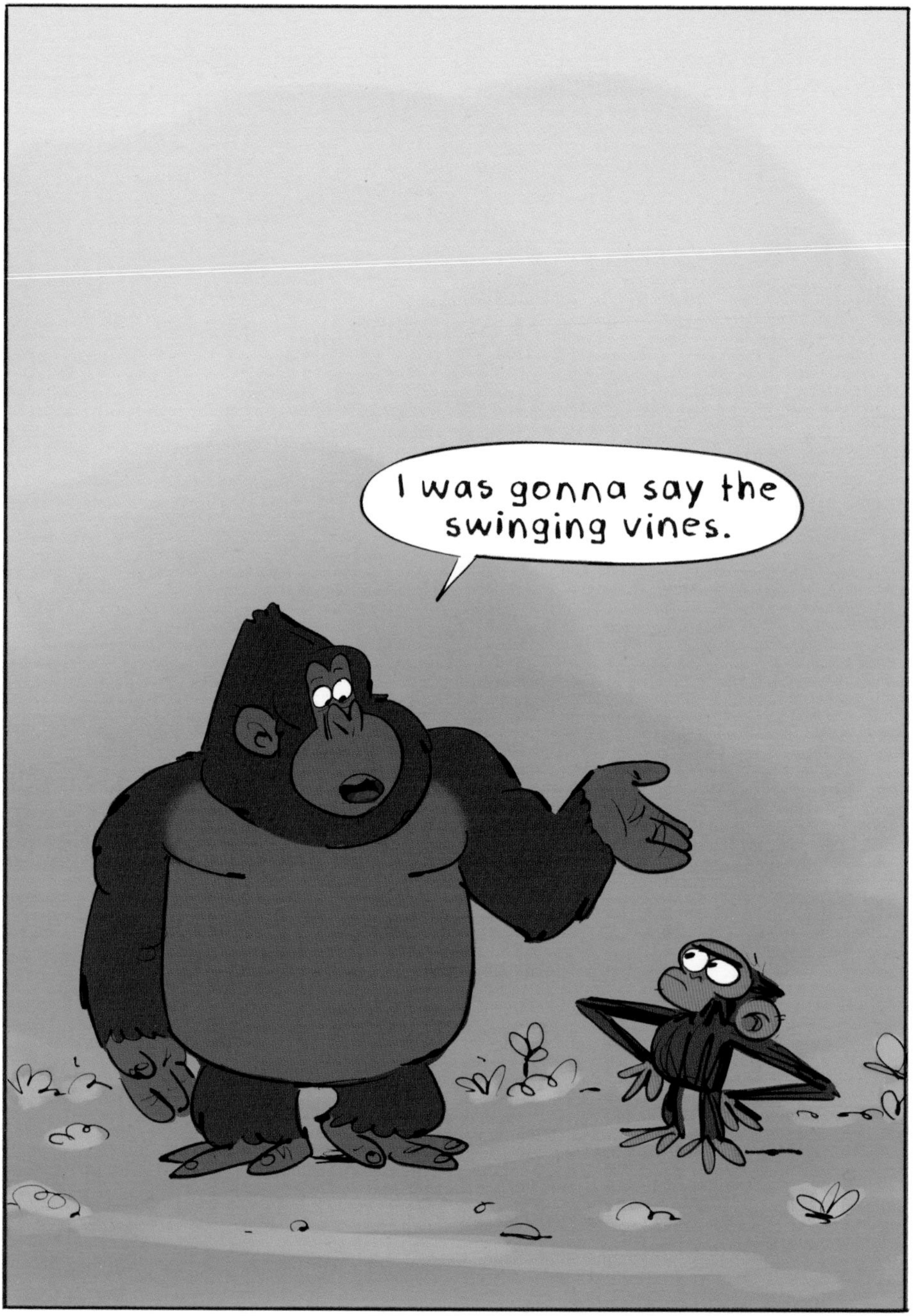
I was gonna say the swinging vines.

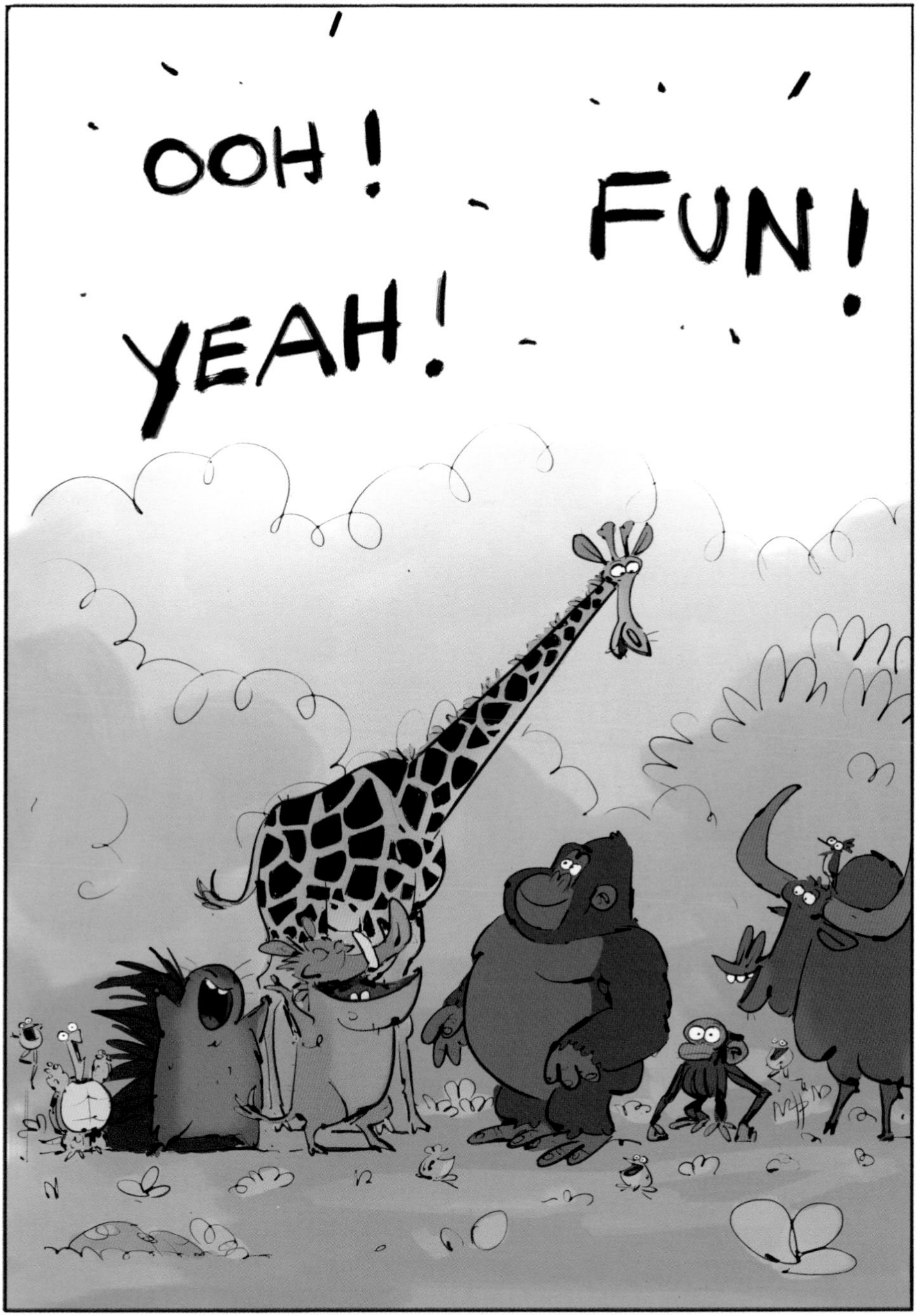
OOH!
FUN!
YEAH!

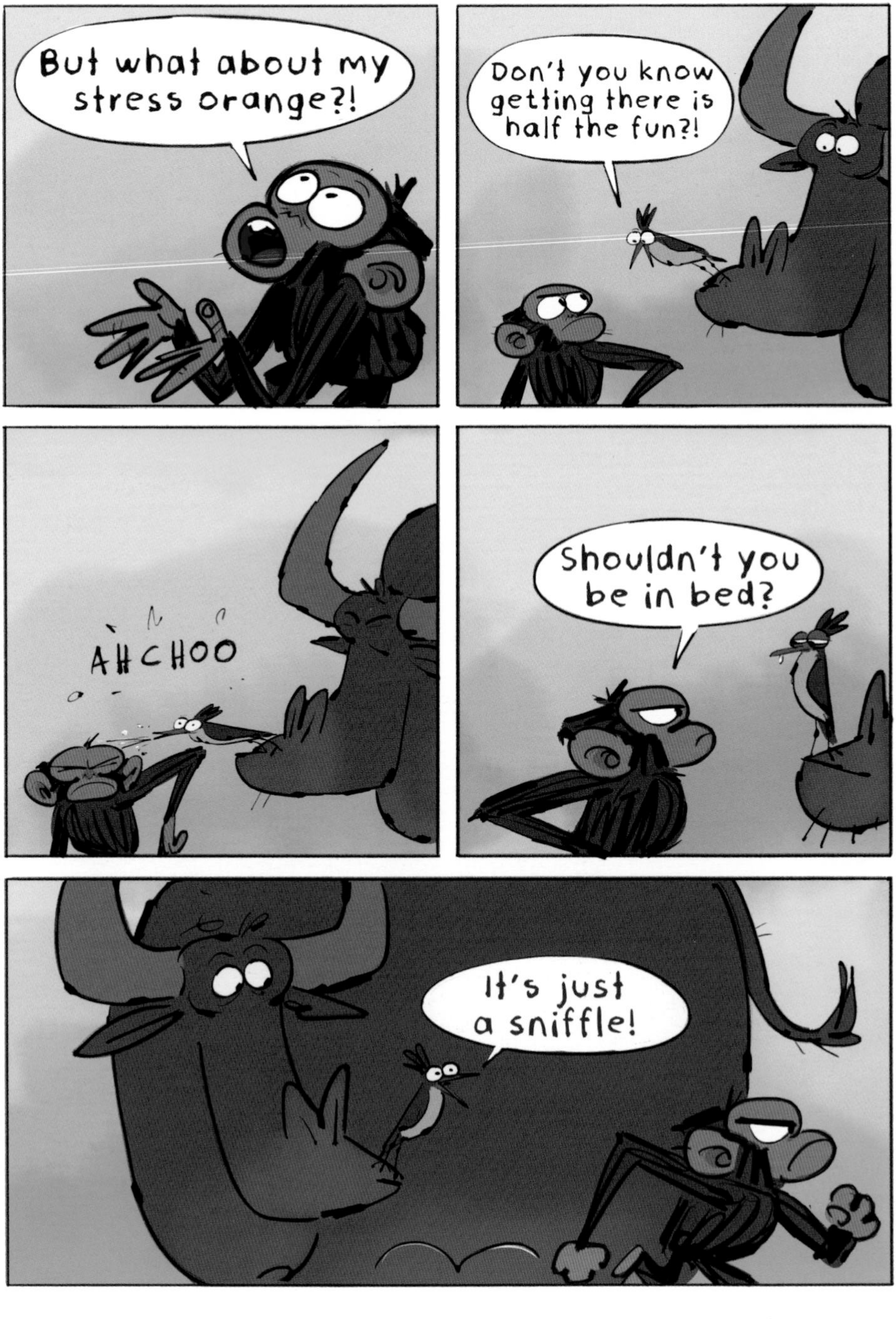
But what about my stress orange?!
Don't you know getting there is half the fun?!
AHCHOO
Shouldn't you be in bed?
It's just a sniffle!

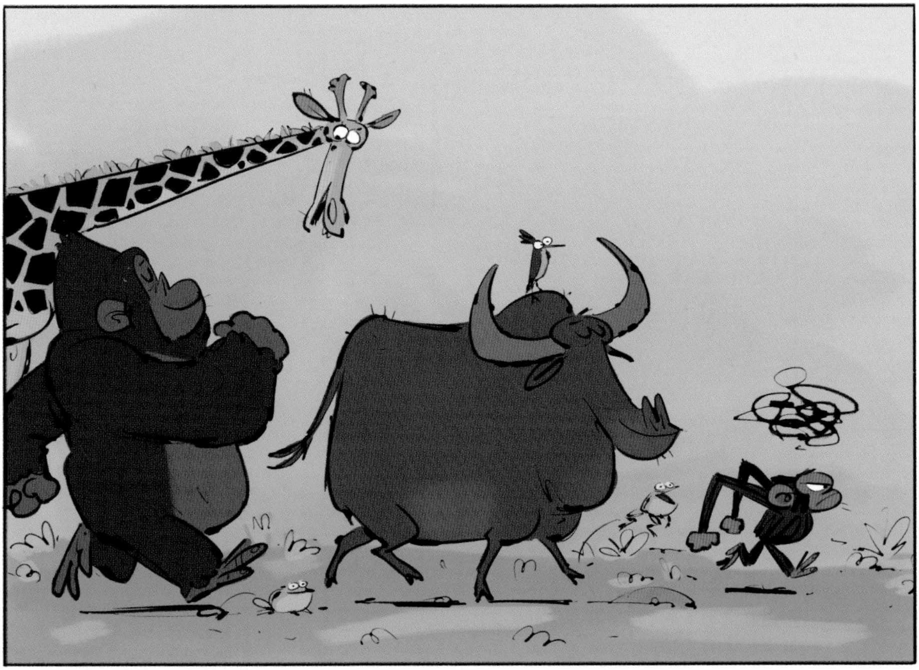

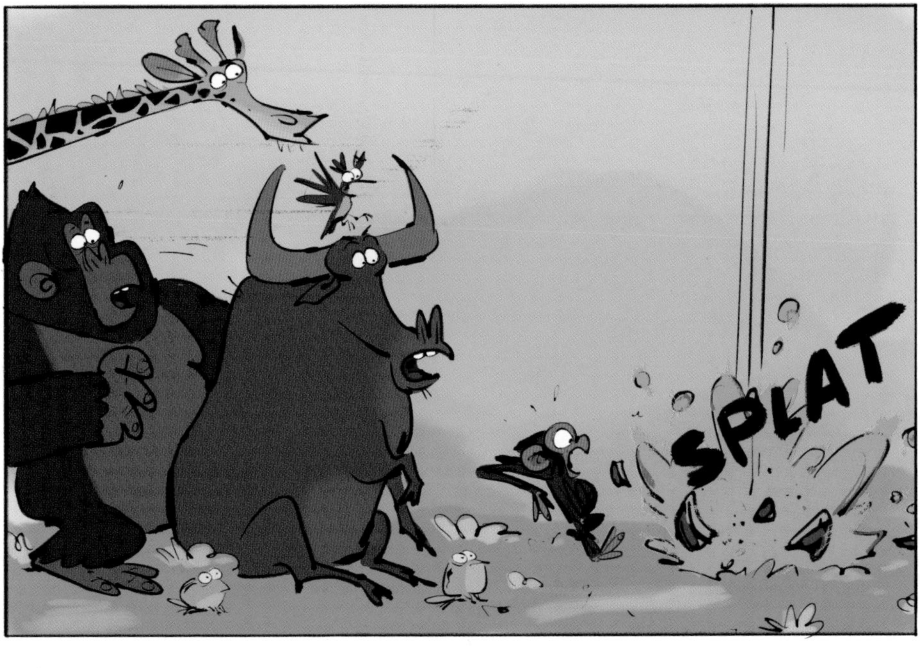
SPLAT

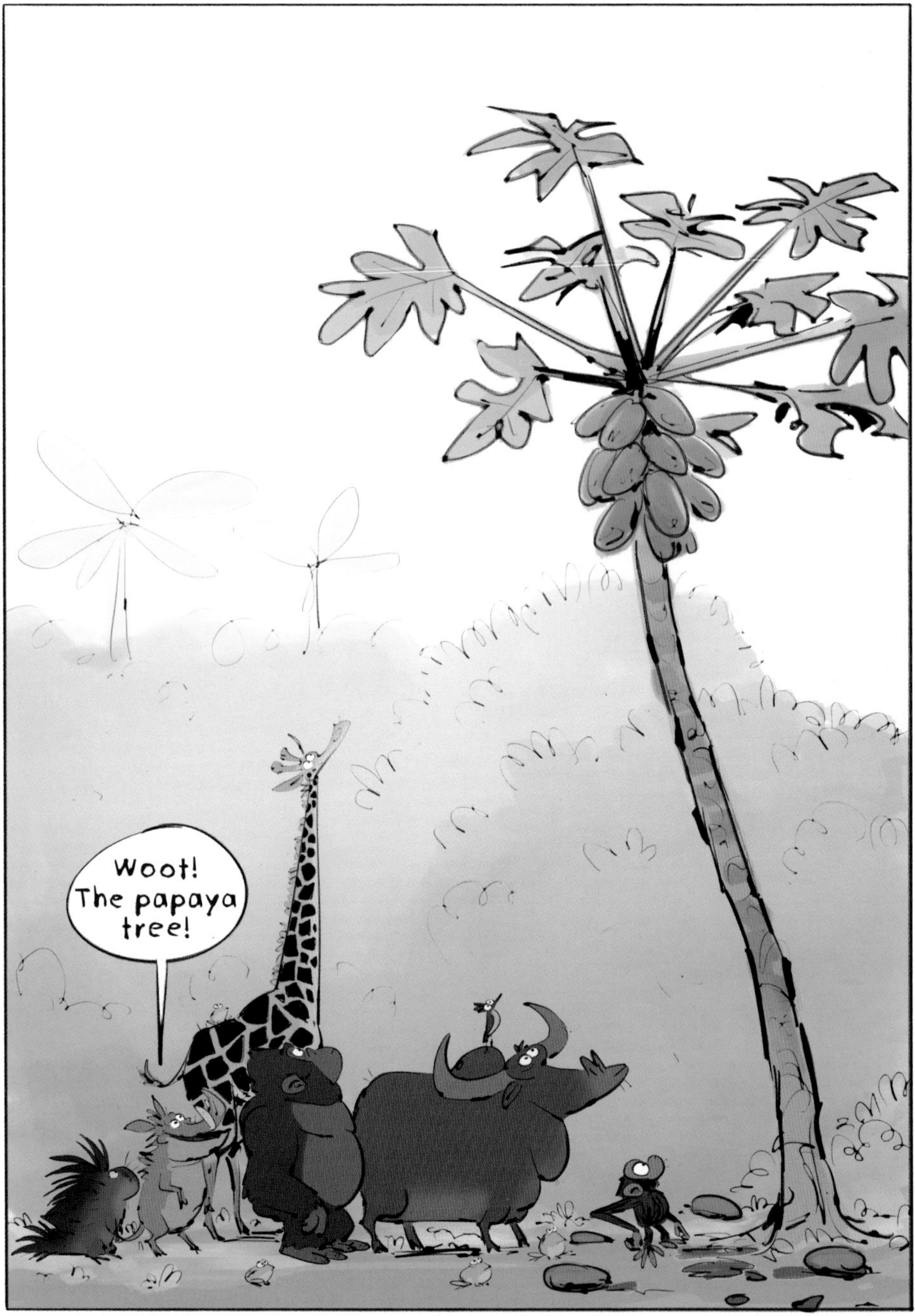
Woot! The papaya tree!

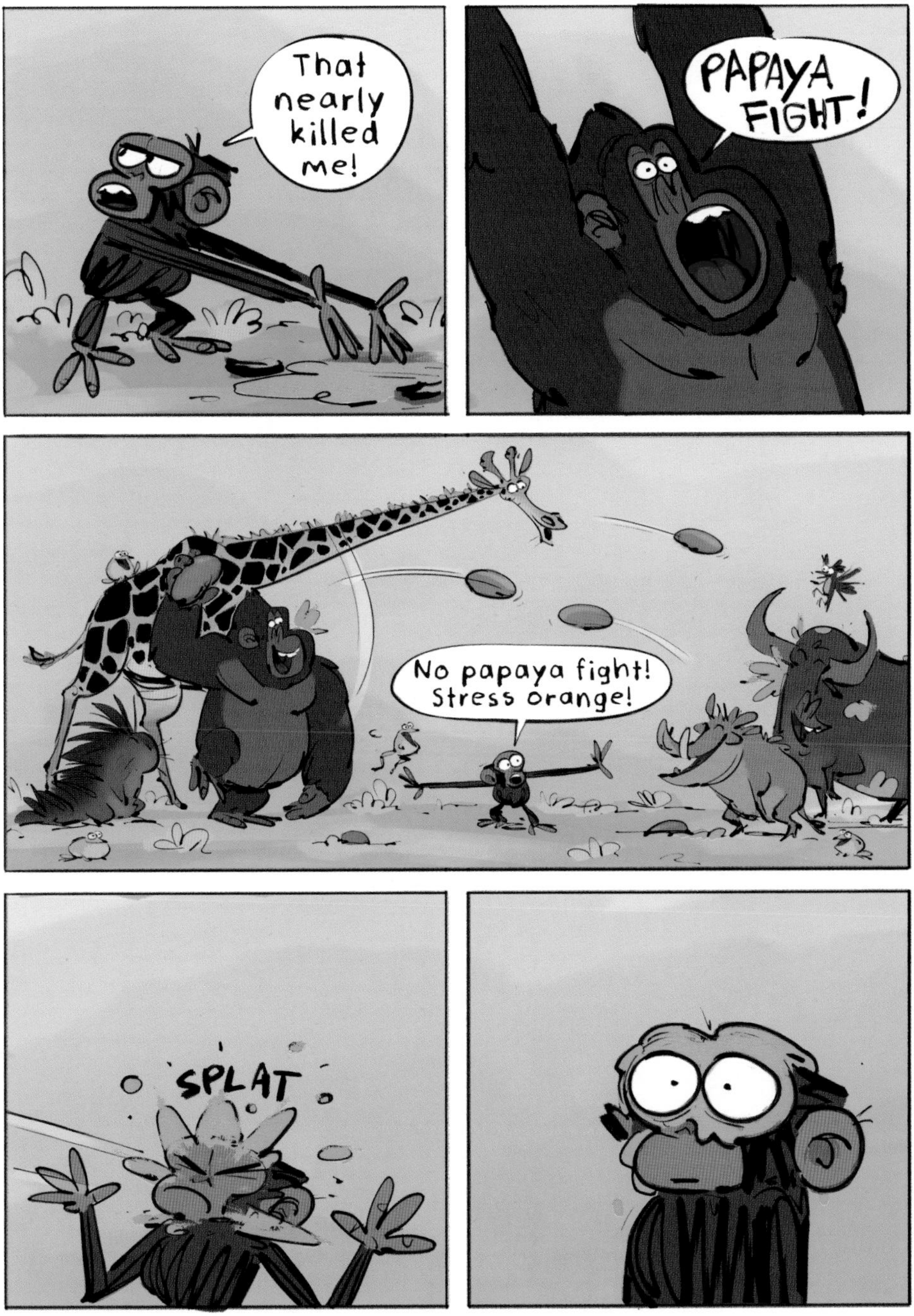
That nearly killed me!
PAPAYA FIGHT!
No papaya fight! Stress orange!
SPLAT

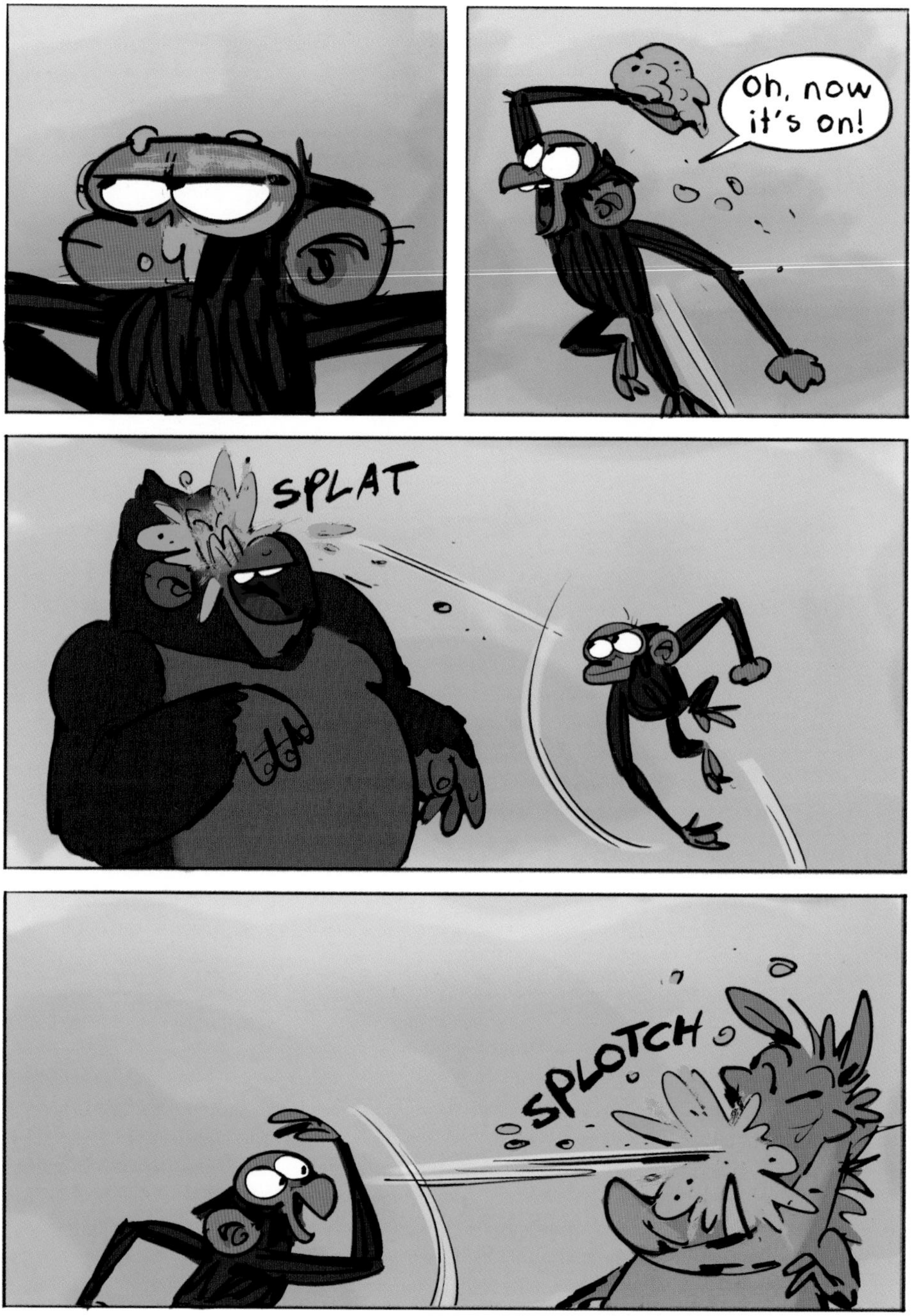
Oh, now it's on!
SPLAT
SPLOTCH

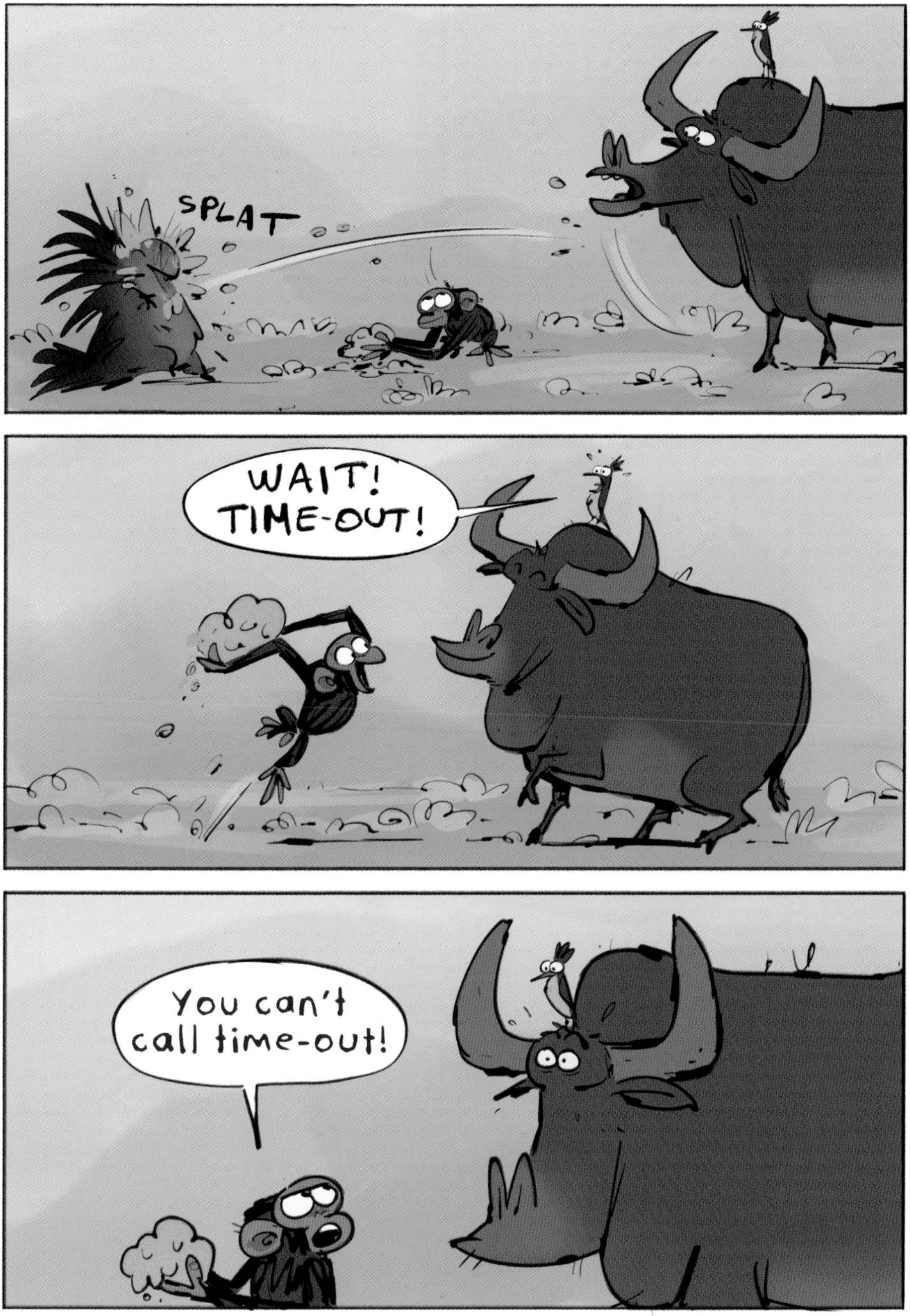
SPLAT
WAIT! TIME-OUT!
You can't call time-out!

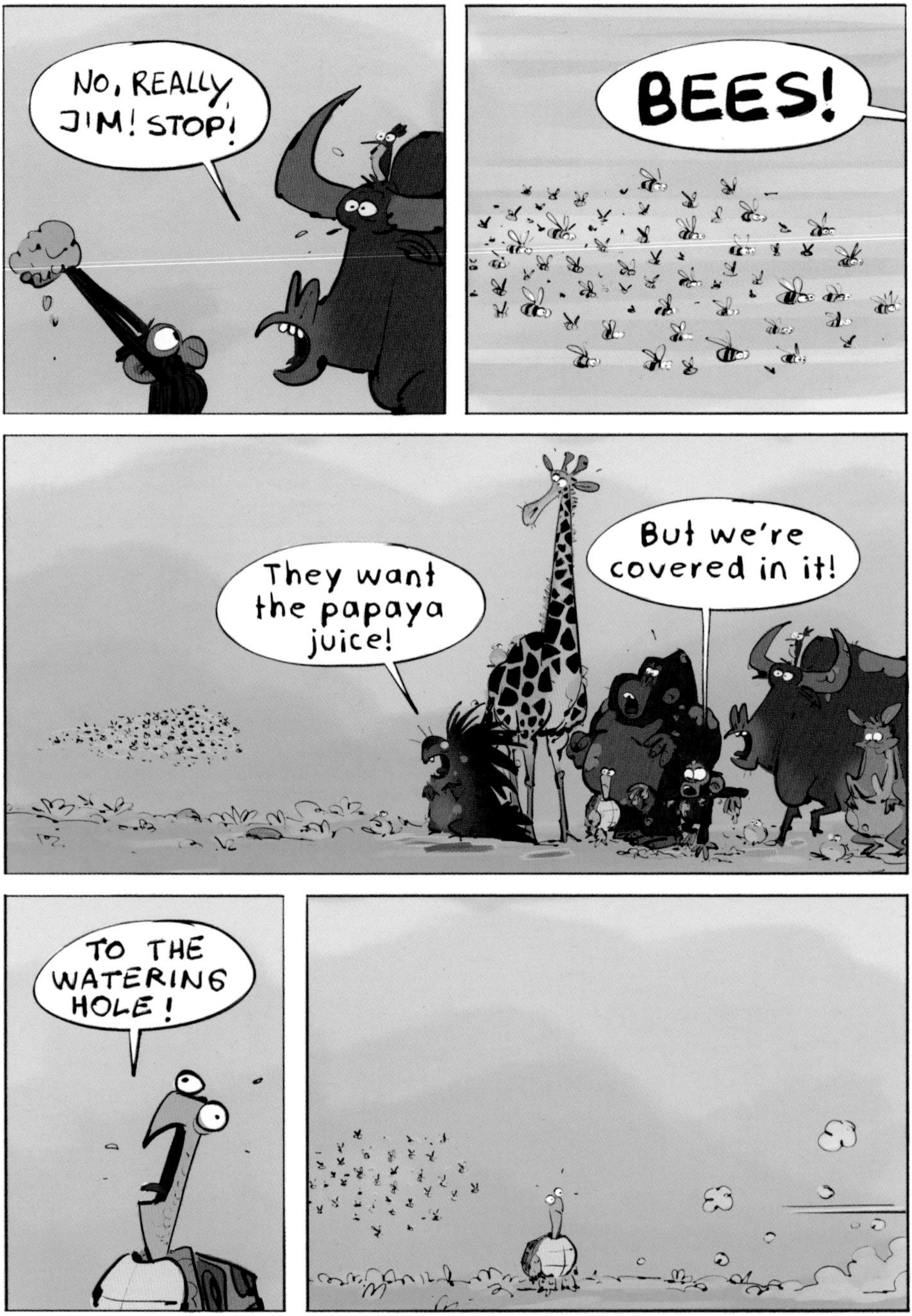
NO, REALLY JIM! STOP!
BEES!
They want the papaya juice!
But we're covered in it!
TO THE WATERING HOLE!

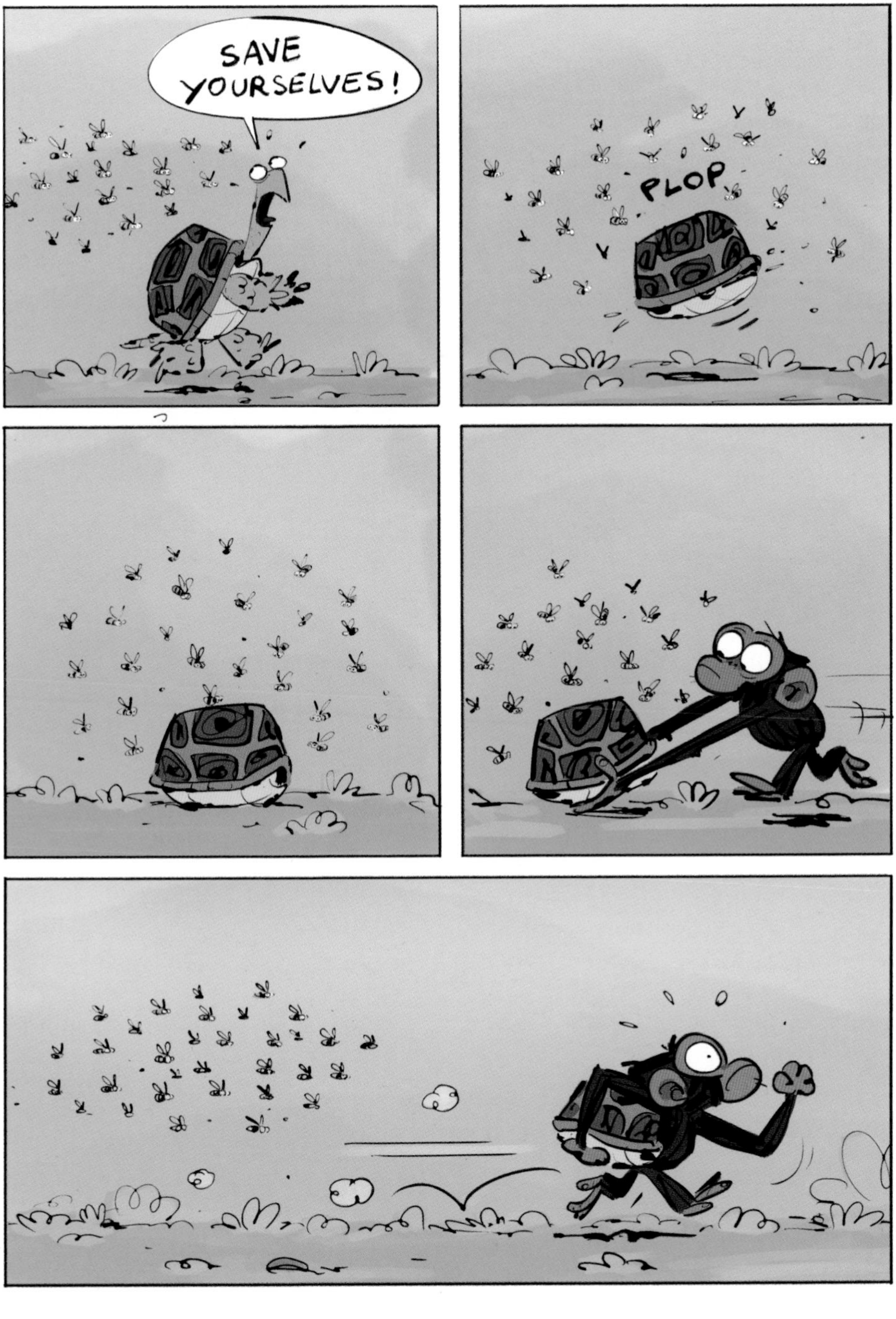
SAVE YOURSELVES!
PLOP

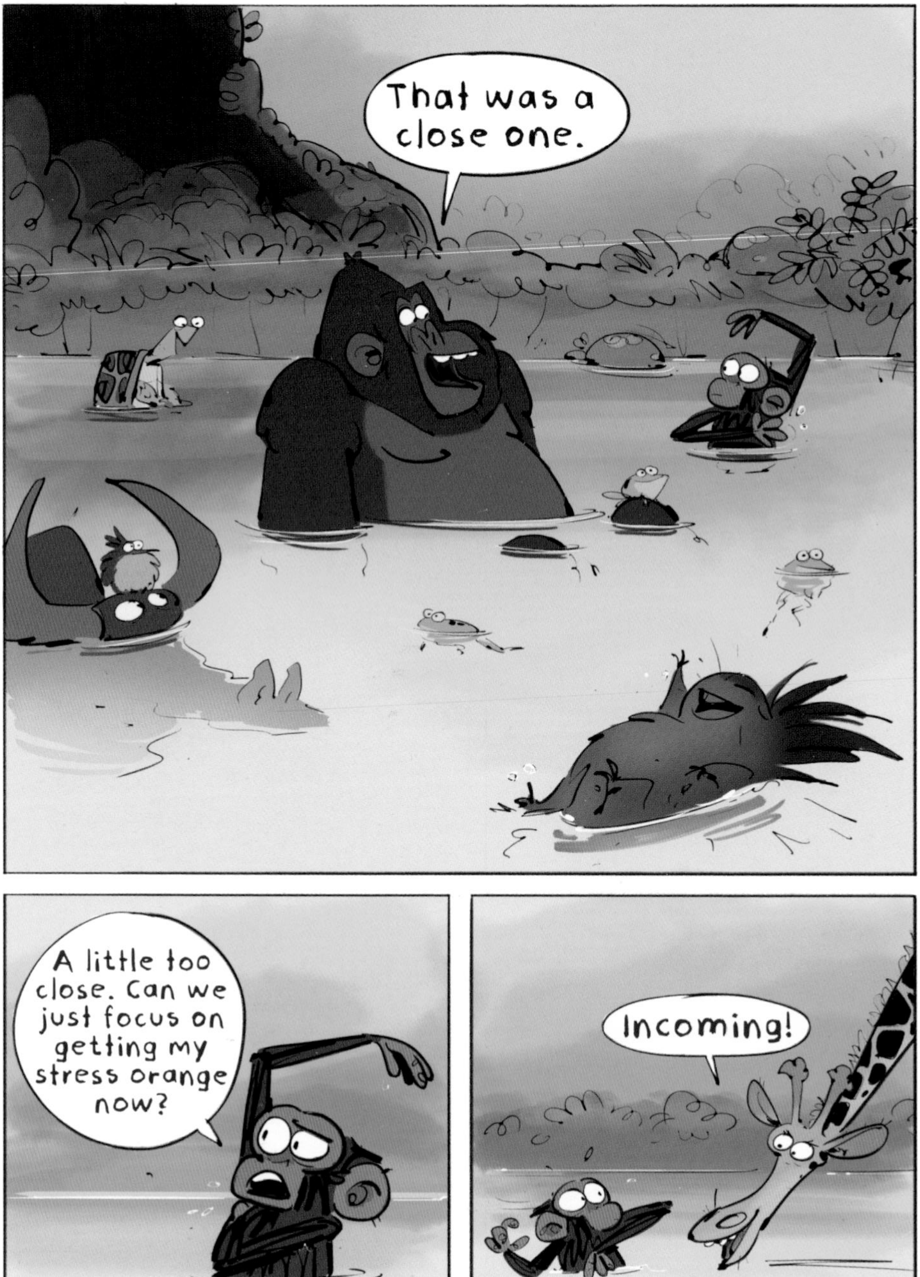
That was a close one.
A little too close. Can we just focus on getting my stress orange now?
Incoming!

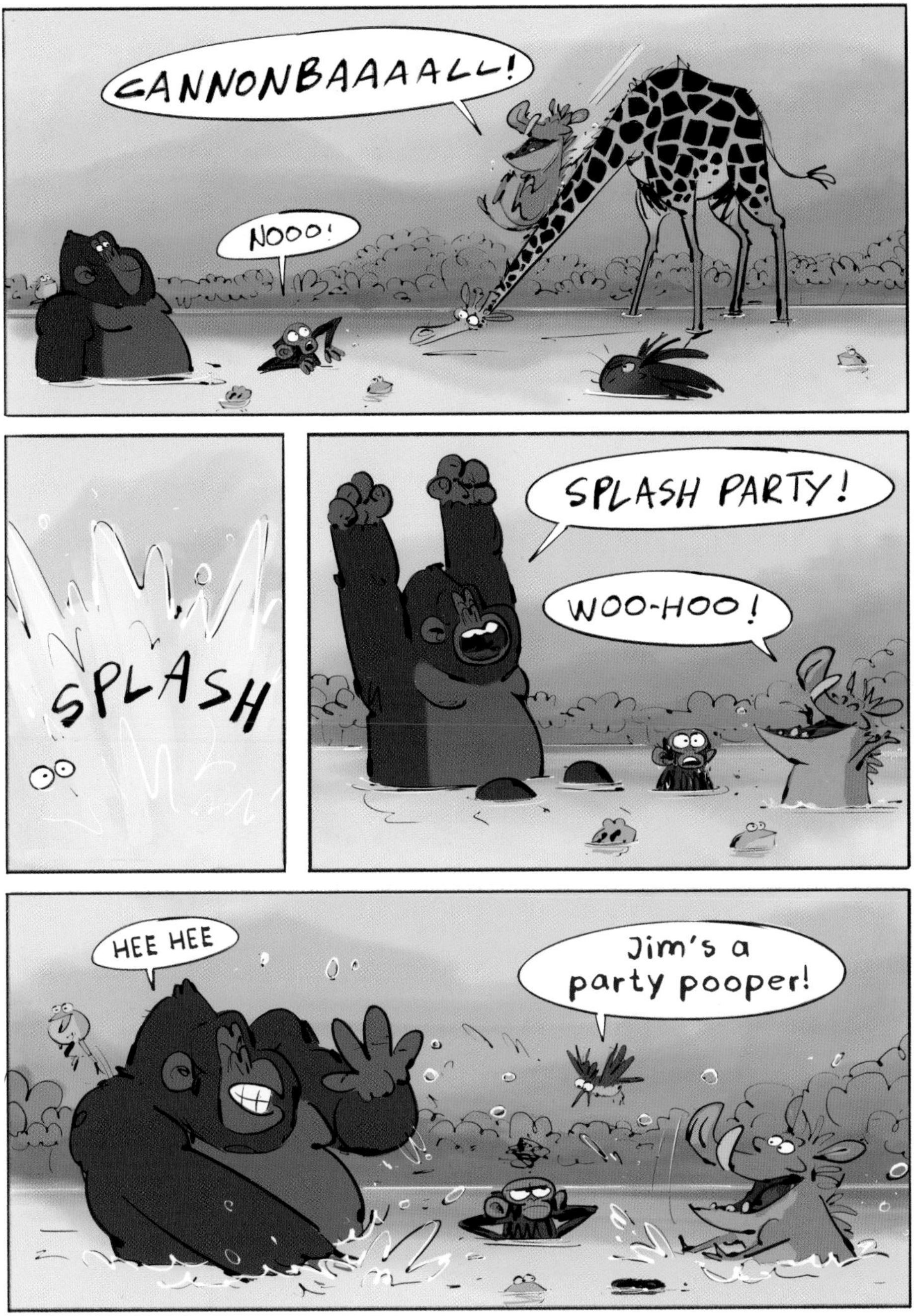
CANNONBAAAALL!
NOOO!
SPLASH
SPLASH PARTY!
WOO-HOO!
HEE HEE
Jim's a party pooper!

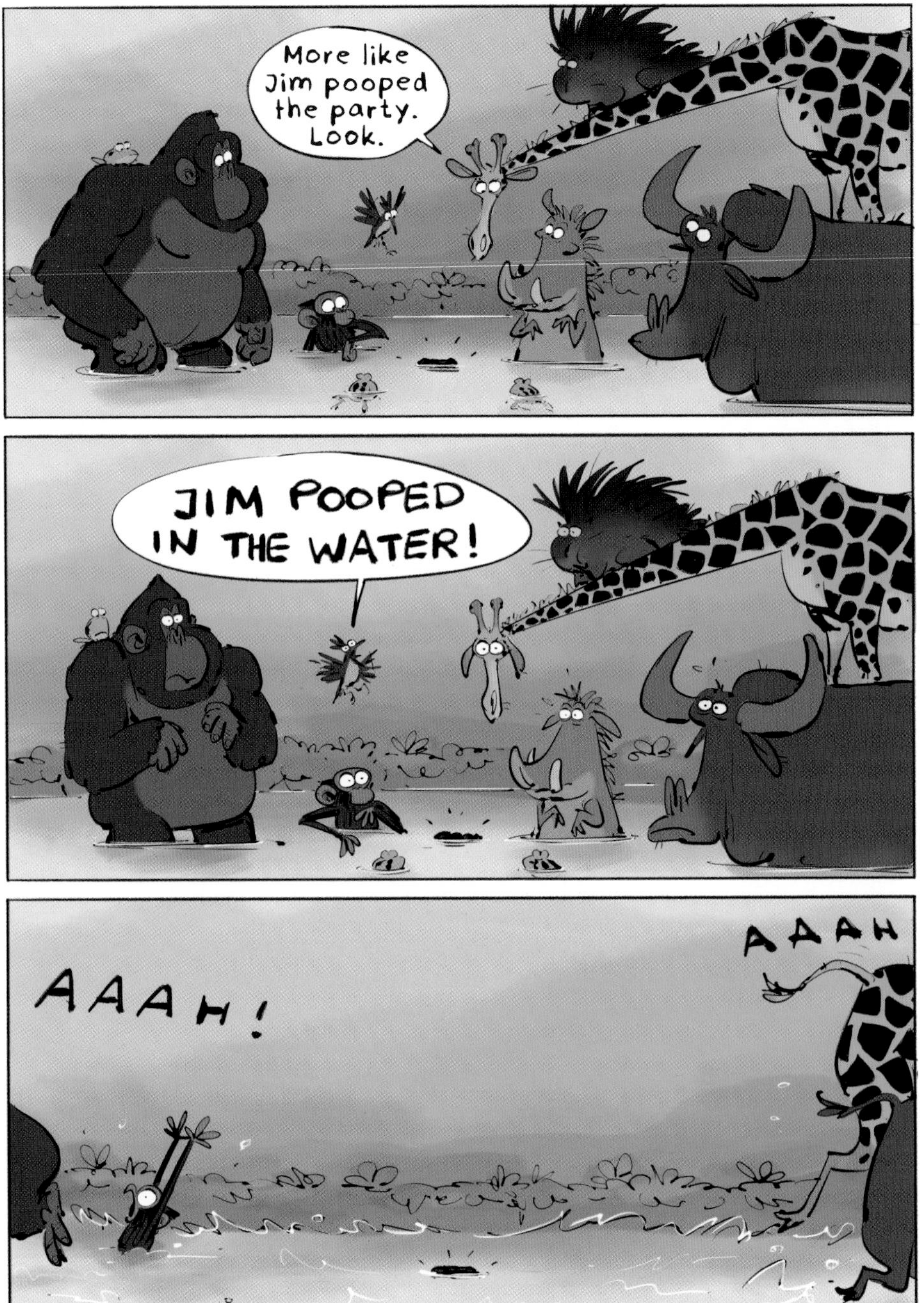
More like Jim pooped the party. Look.
JIM POOPED IN THE WATER!
AAAH!
AAAH

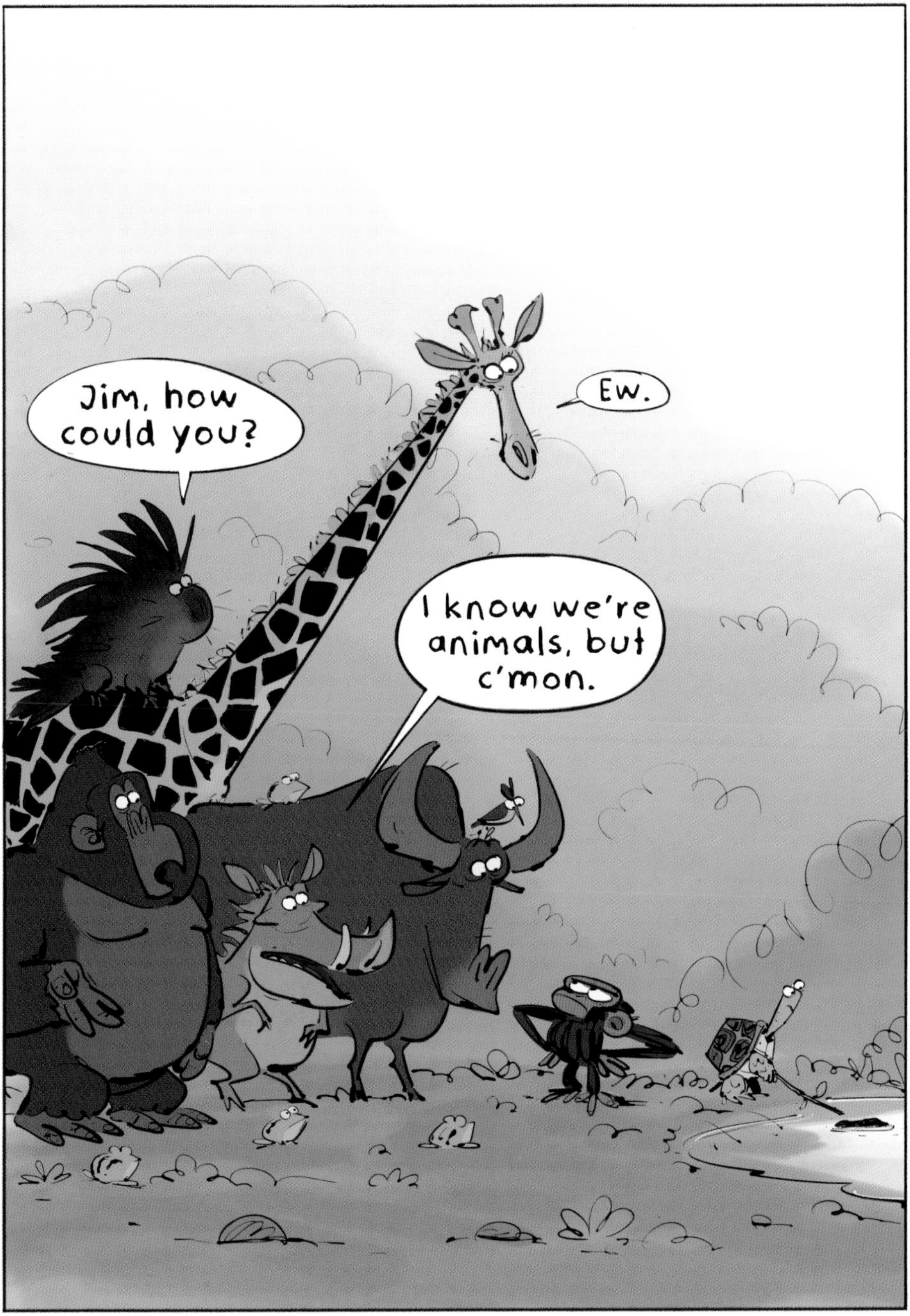
Jim, how could you?
Ew.
I know we're animals, but c'mon.

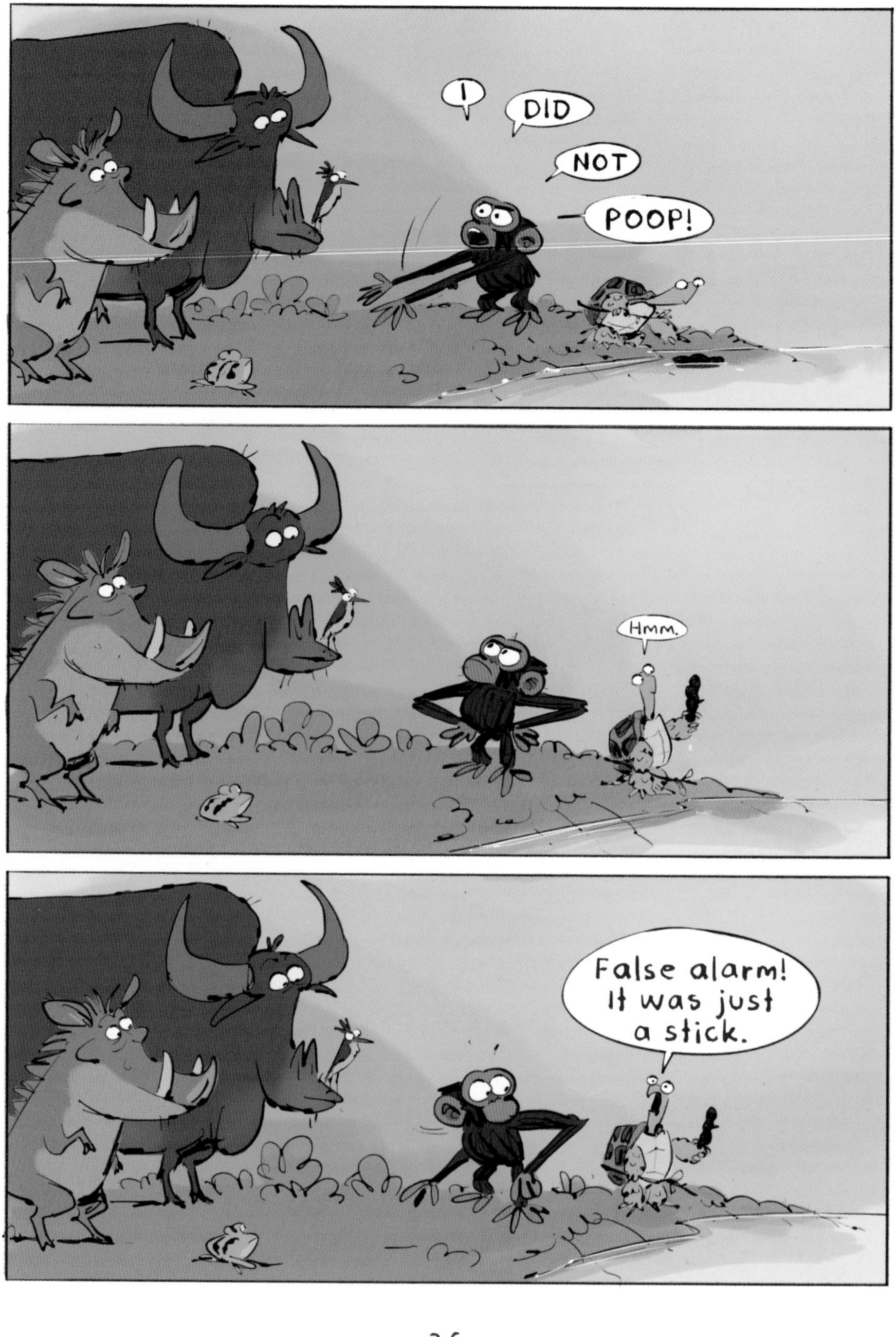
I
DID
NOT
POOP!
Hmm.
False alarm! It was just a stick.

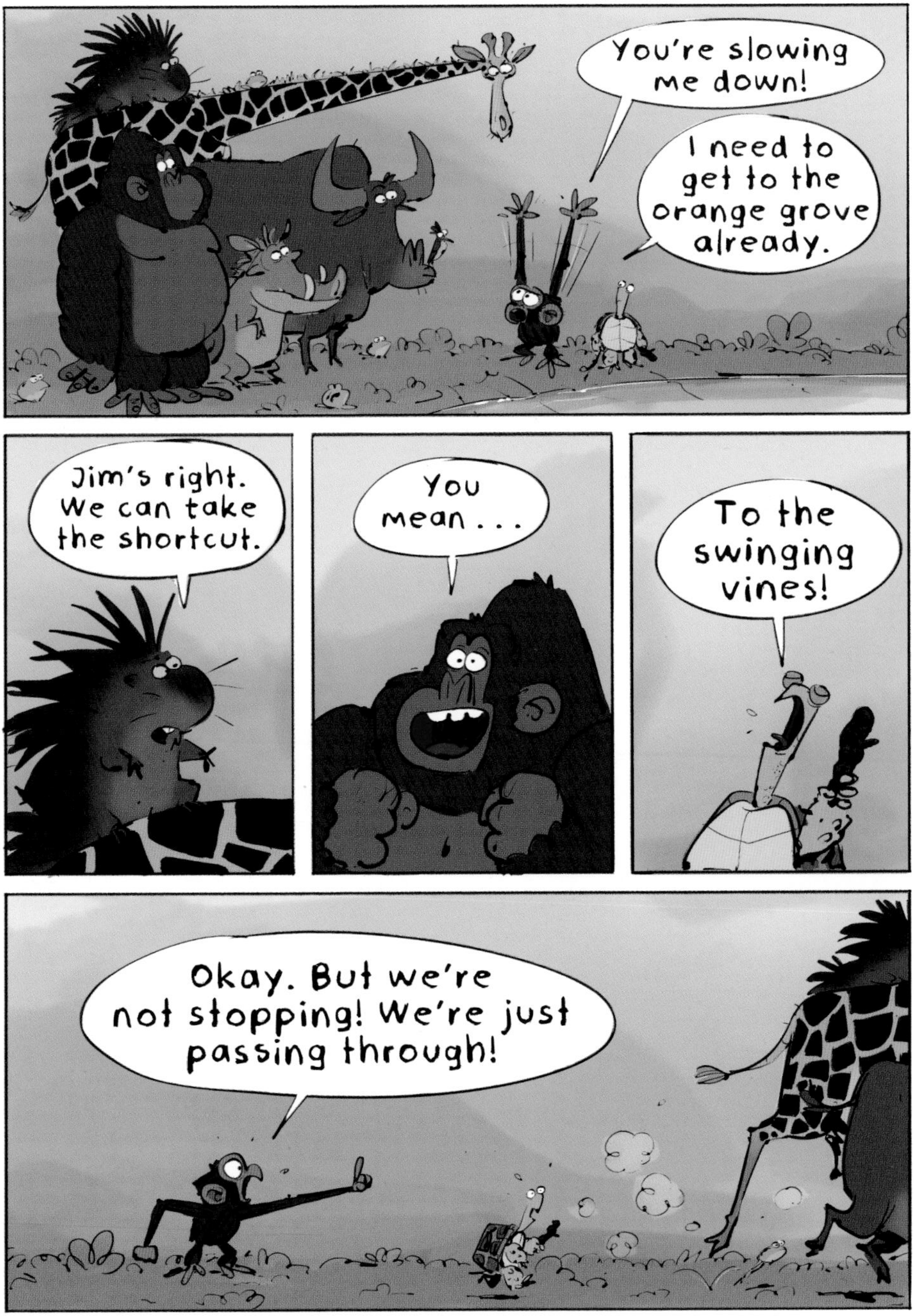
You're slowing me down!
I need to get to the orange grove already.
Jim's right. We can take the shortcut.
You mean . . .
To the swinging vines!
Okay. But we're not stopping! We're just passing through!

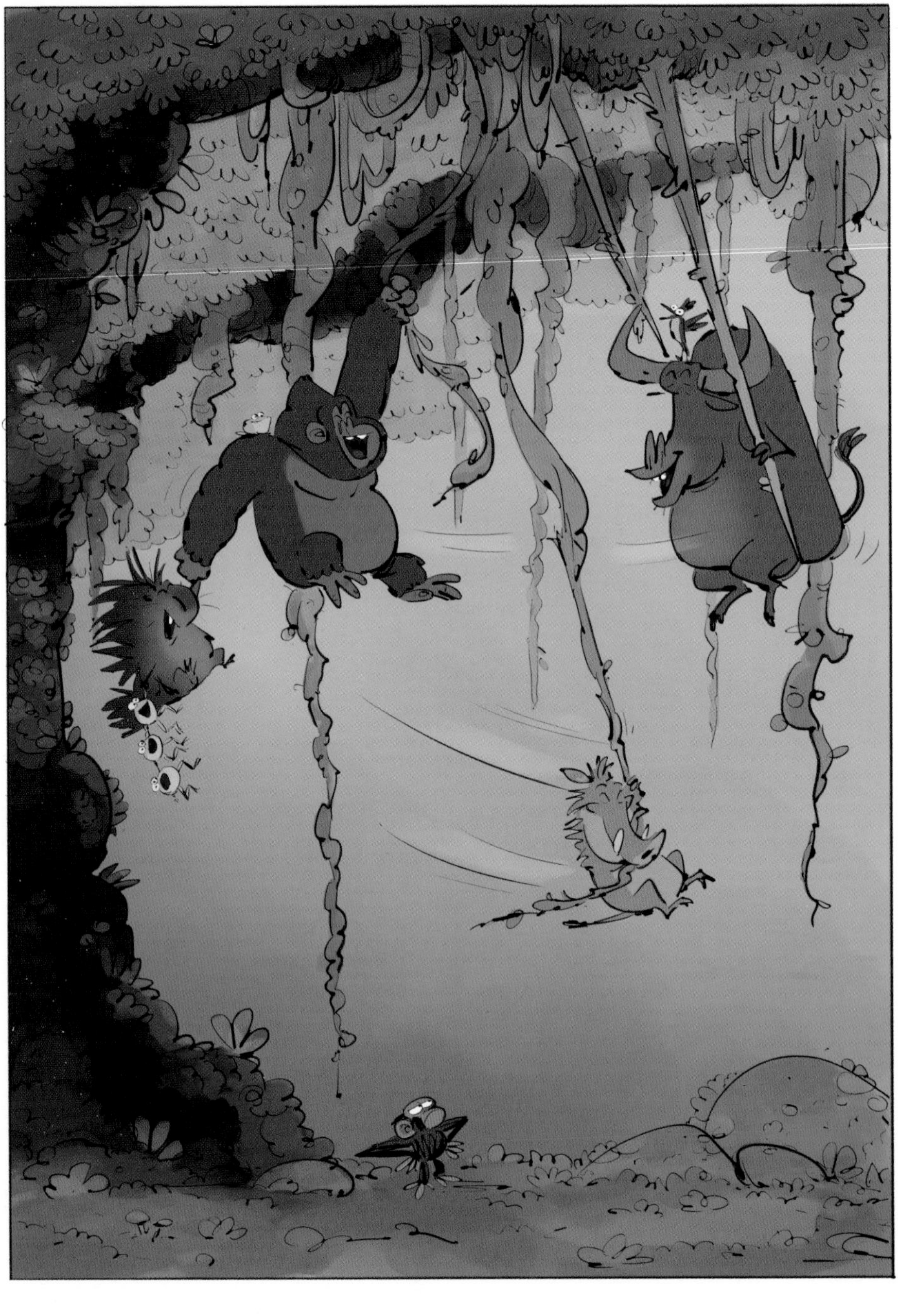

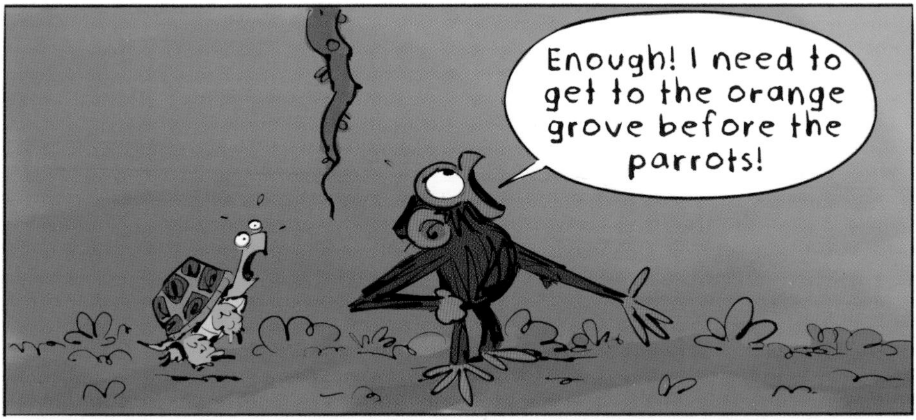
Enough! I need to get to the orange grove before the parrots!

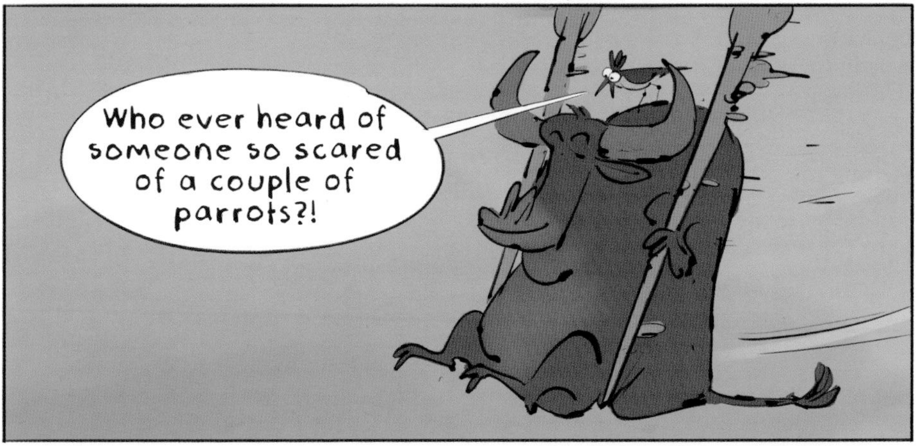
Who ever heard of someone so scared of a couple of parrots?!

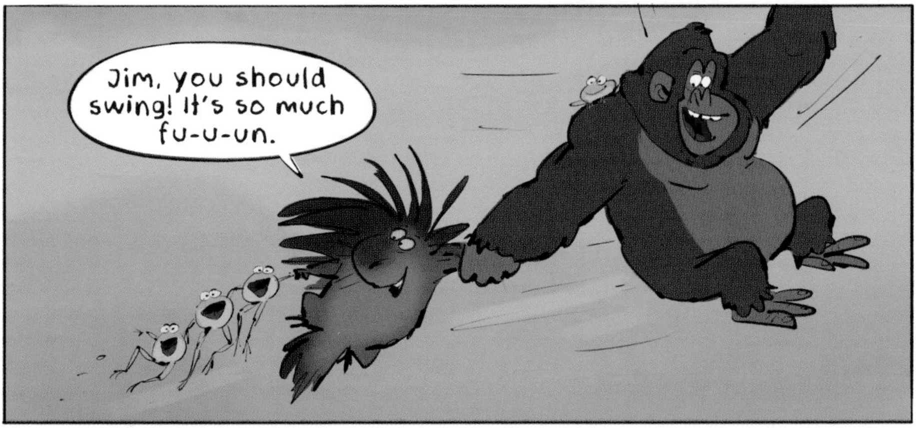
Jim, you should swing! It's so much fu-u-un.

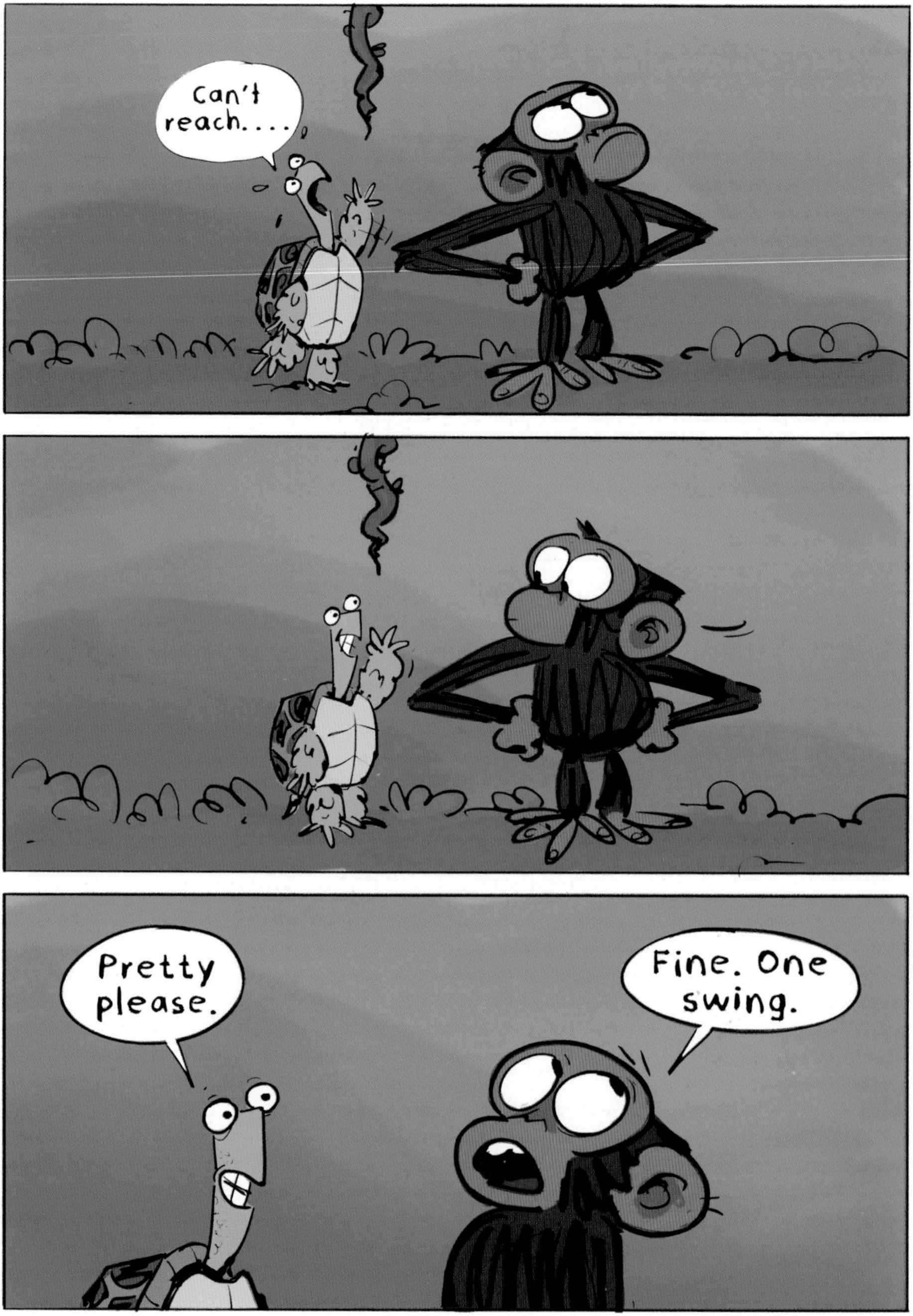
Can't reach....
Pretty please.
Fine. One swing.

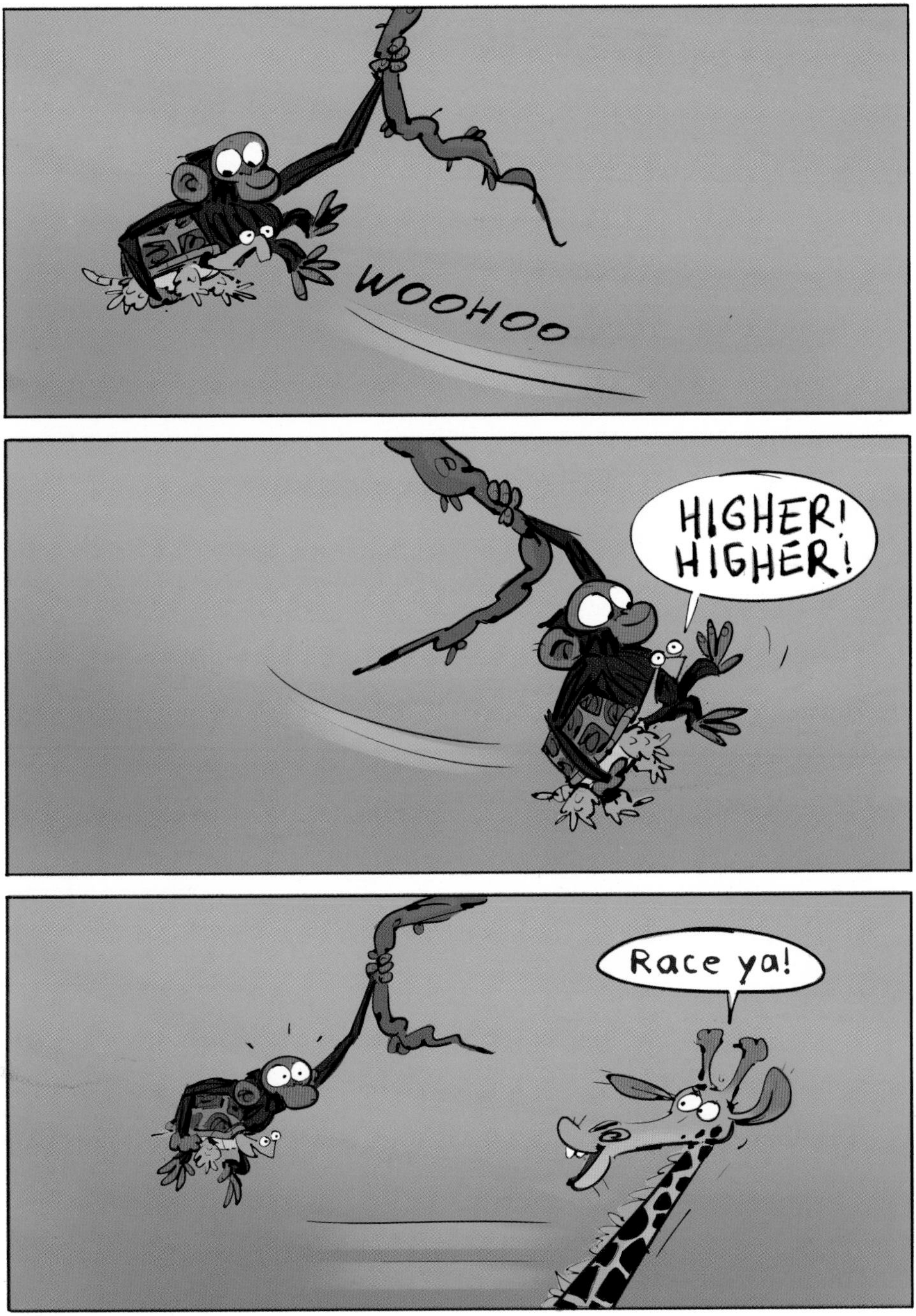
WOOHOO
HIGHER! HIGHER!
Race ya!

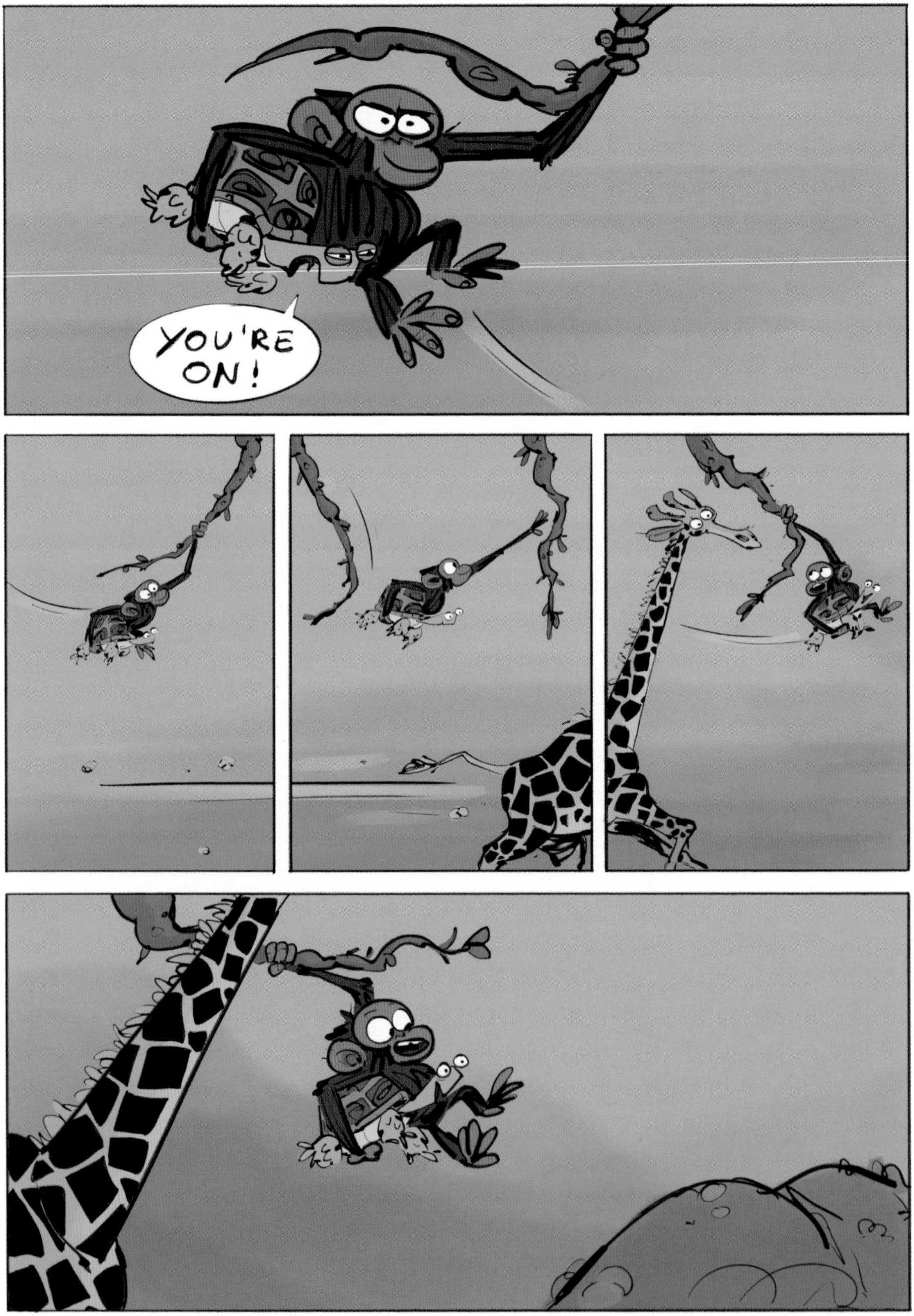
YOU'RE ON!

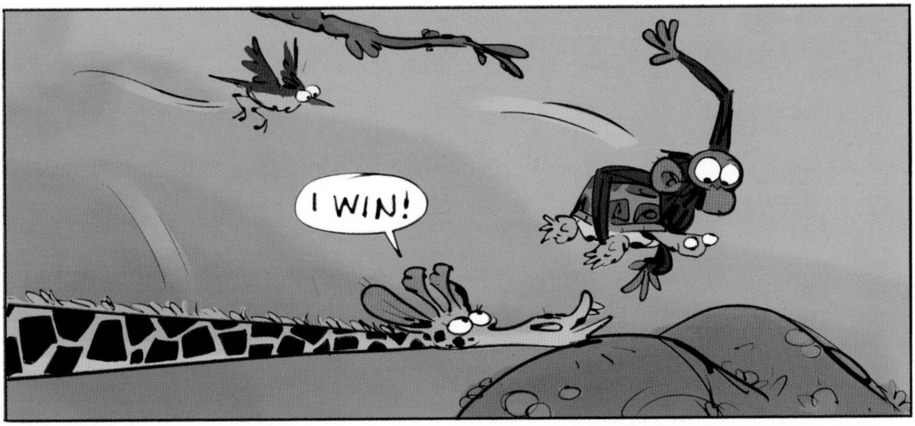
I WIN!

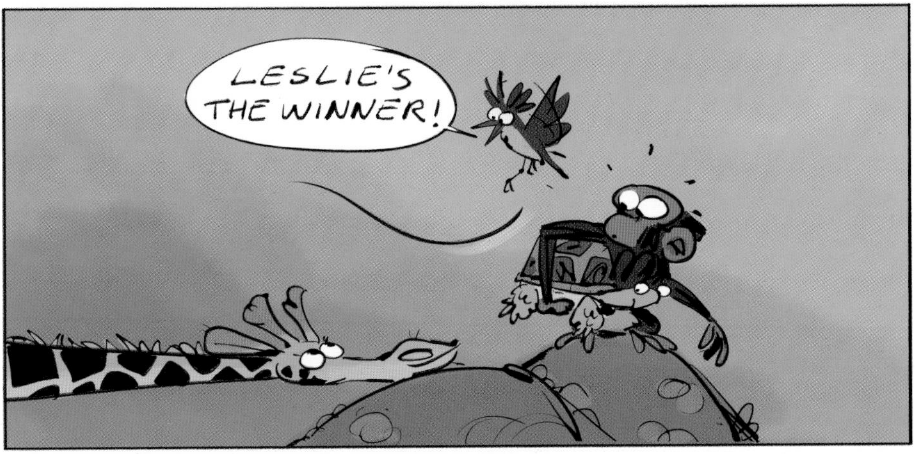
LESLIE'S THE WINNER!

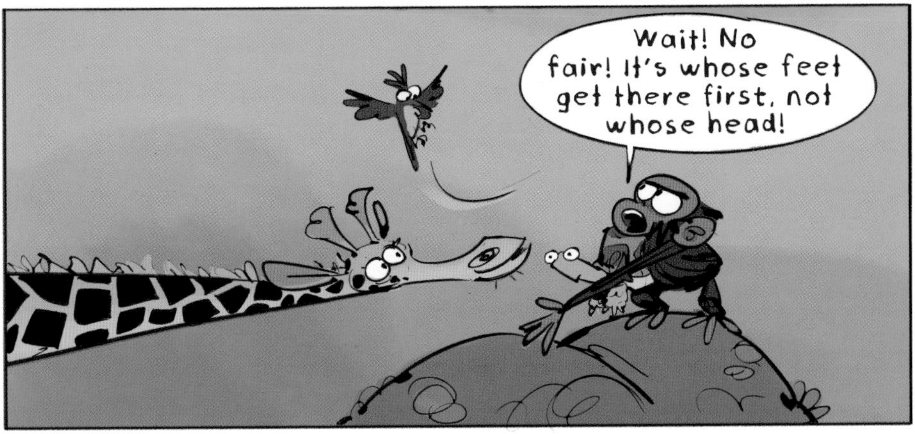
Wait! No fair! It's whose feet get there first, not whose head!

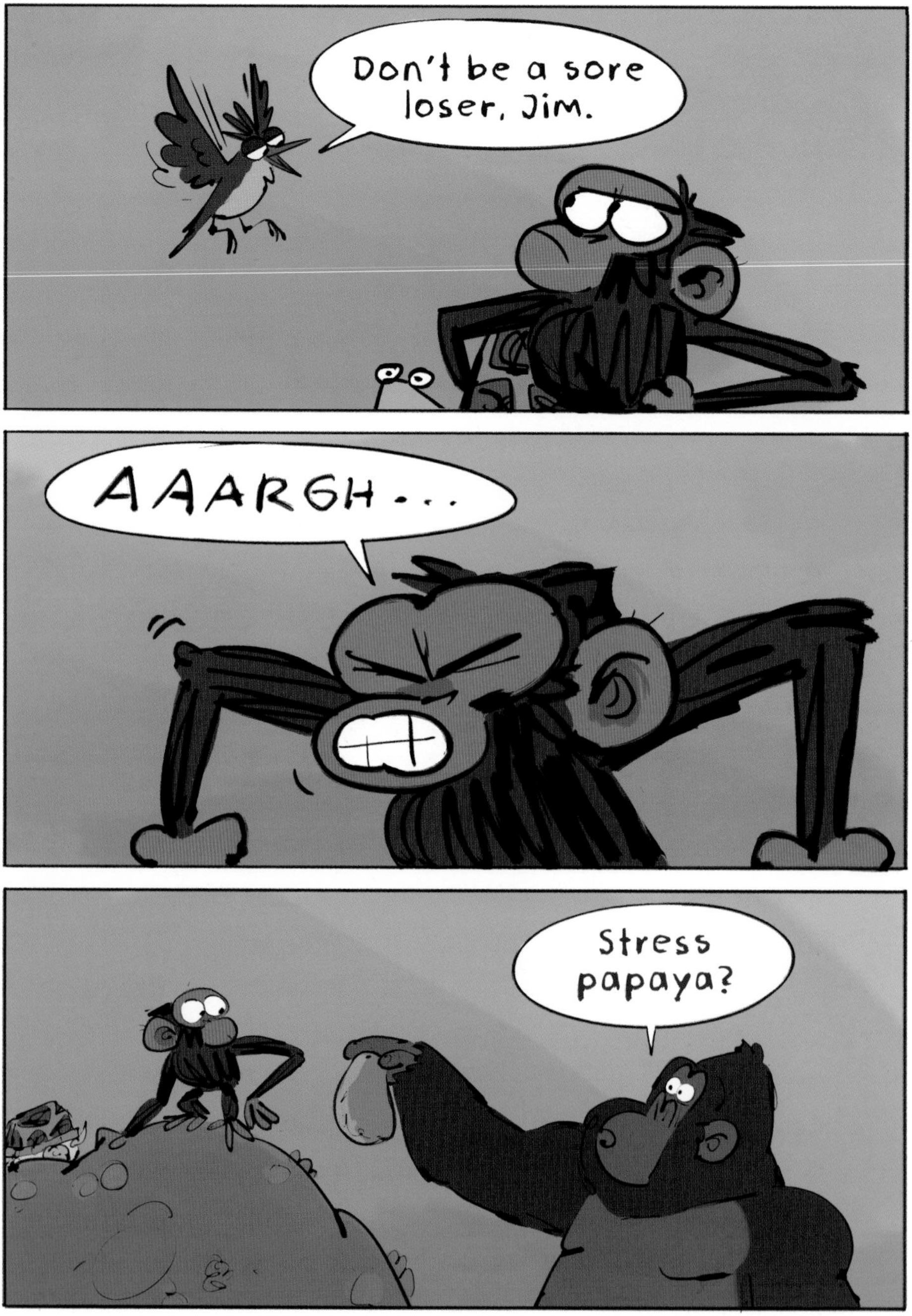

Don't be a sore loser, Jim.
AAARGH...
Stress papaya?

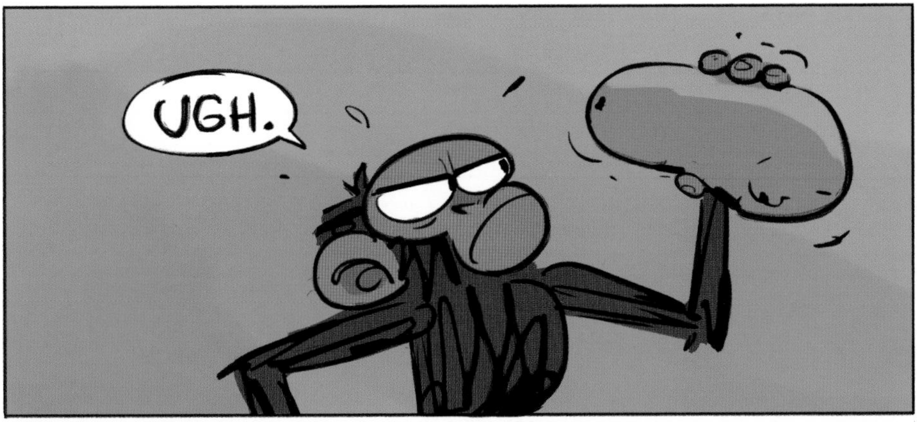
UGH.
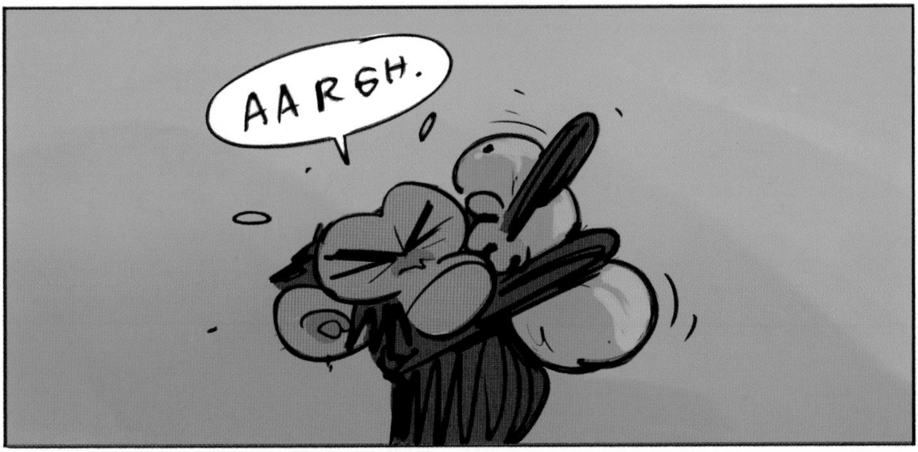
AARGH.
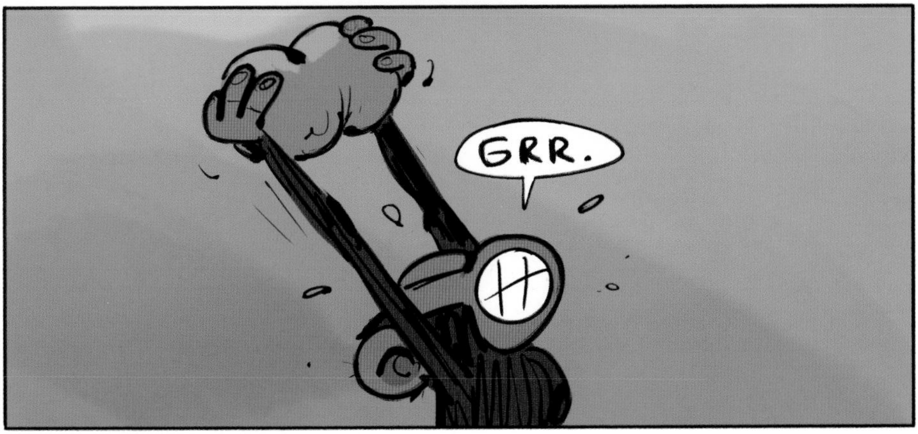
GRR.

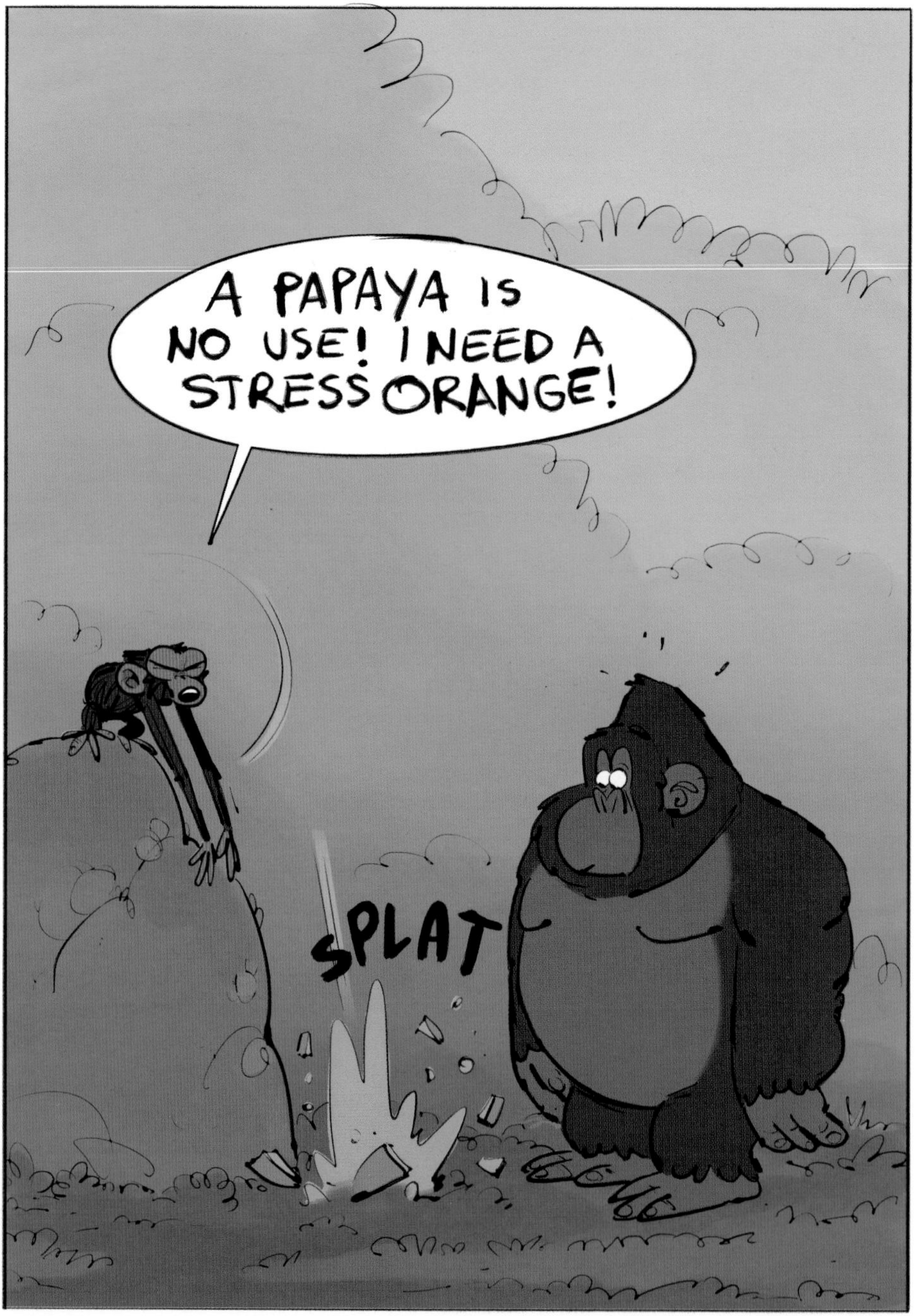
A PAPAYA IS NO USE! I NEED A STRESS ORANGE!
SPLAT

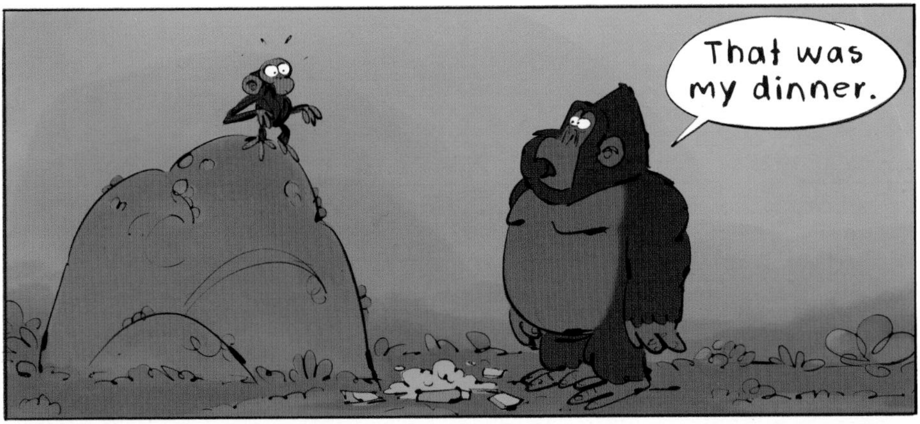
That was my dinner.

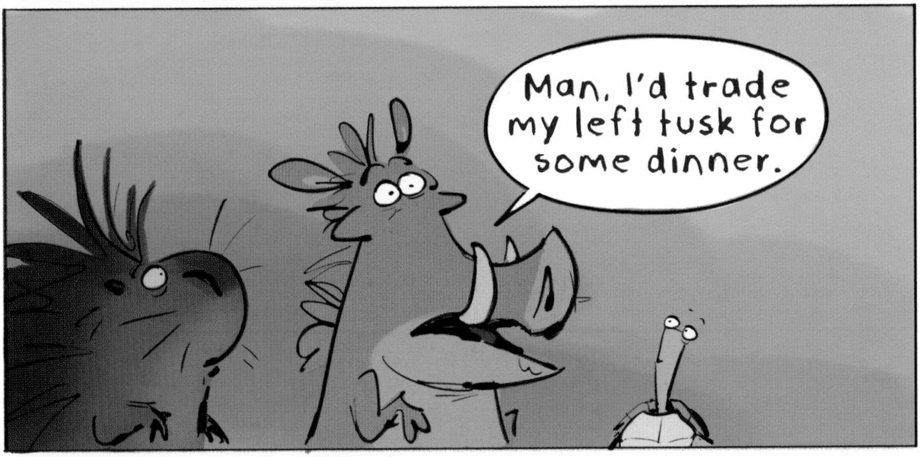
Man, I'd trade my left tusk for some dinner.

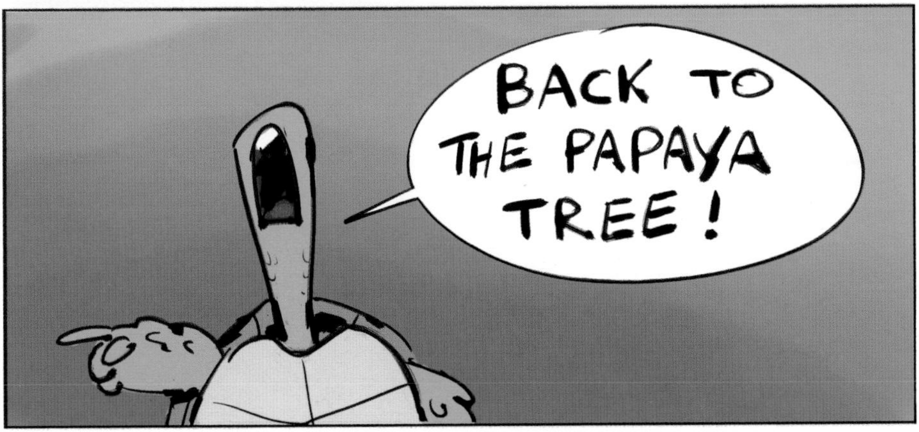
BACK TO THE PAPAYA TREE!

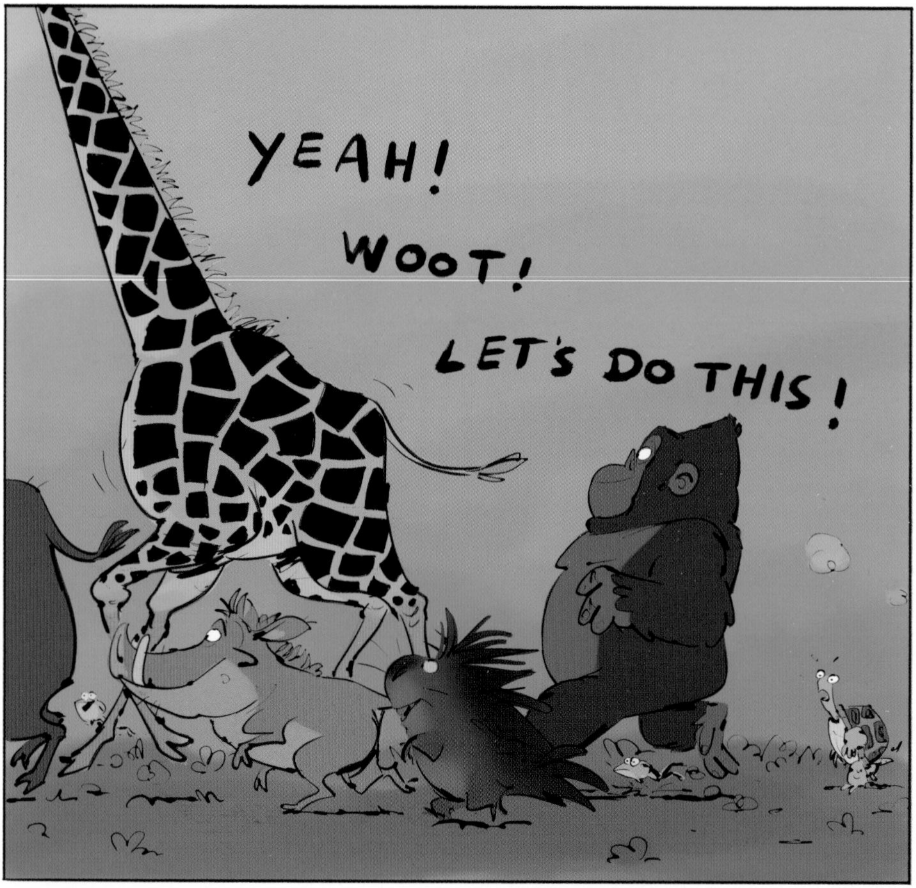
YEAH!
WOOT!
LET'S DO THIS!

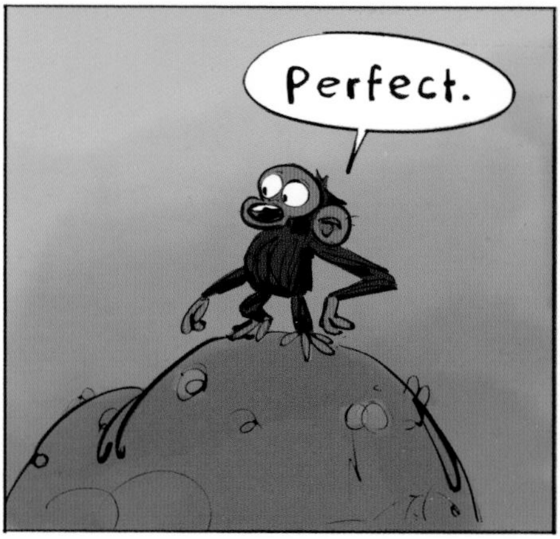
Perfect.

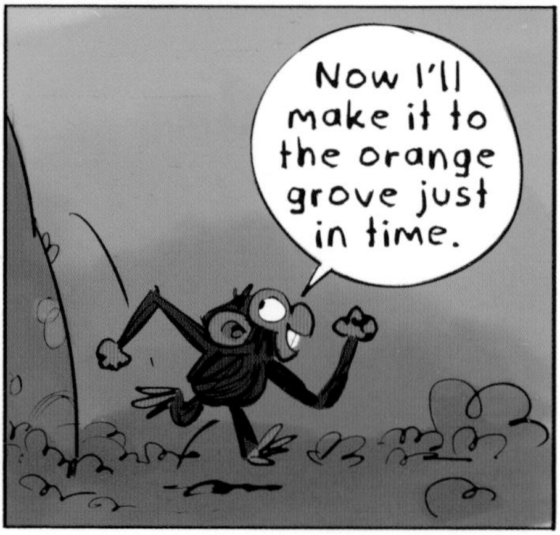
Now I'll make it to the orange grove just in time.

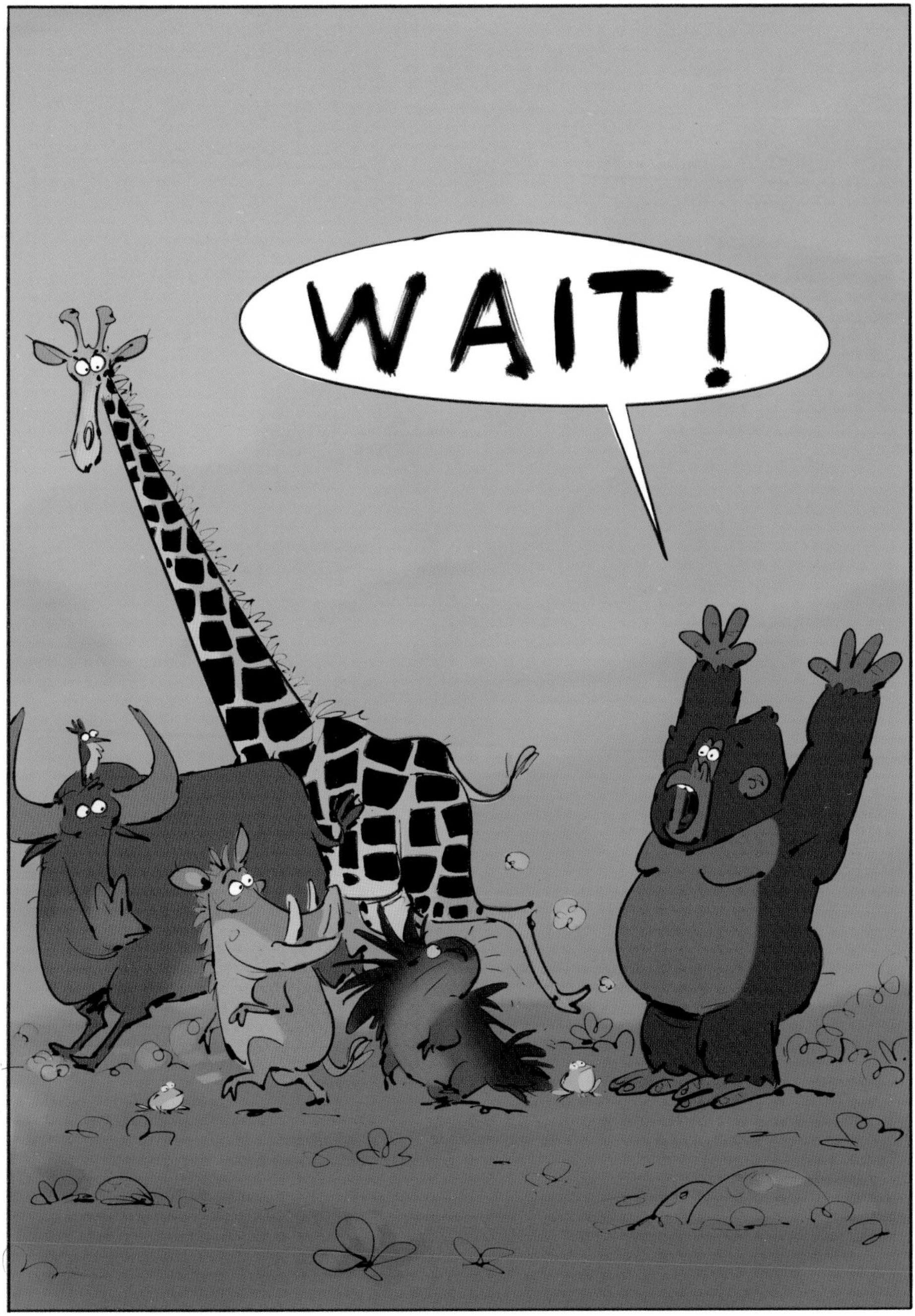
WAIT!

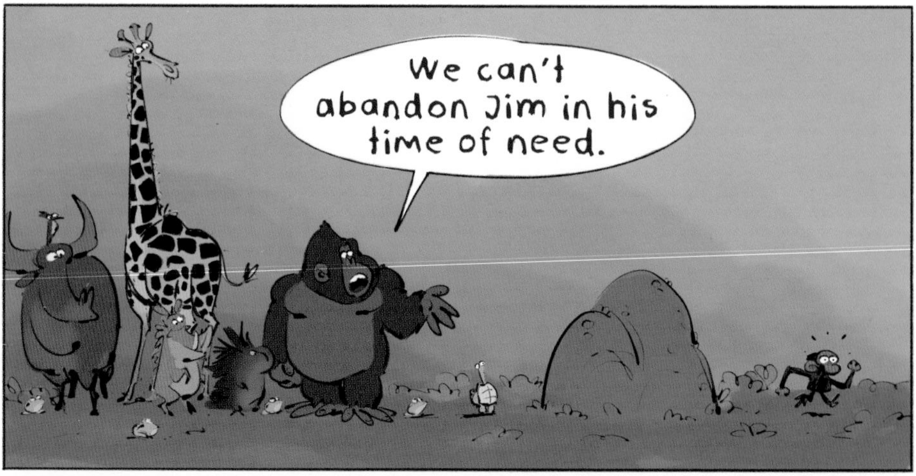
We can't abandon Jim in his time of need.

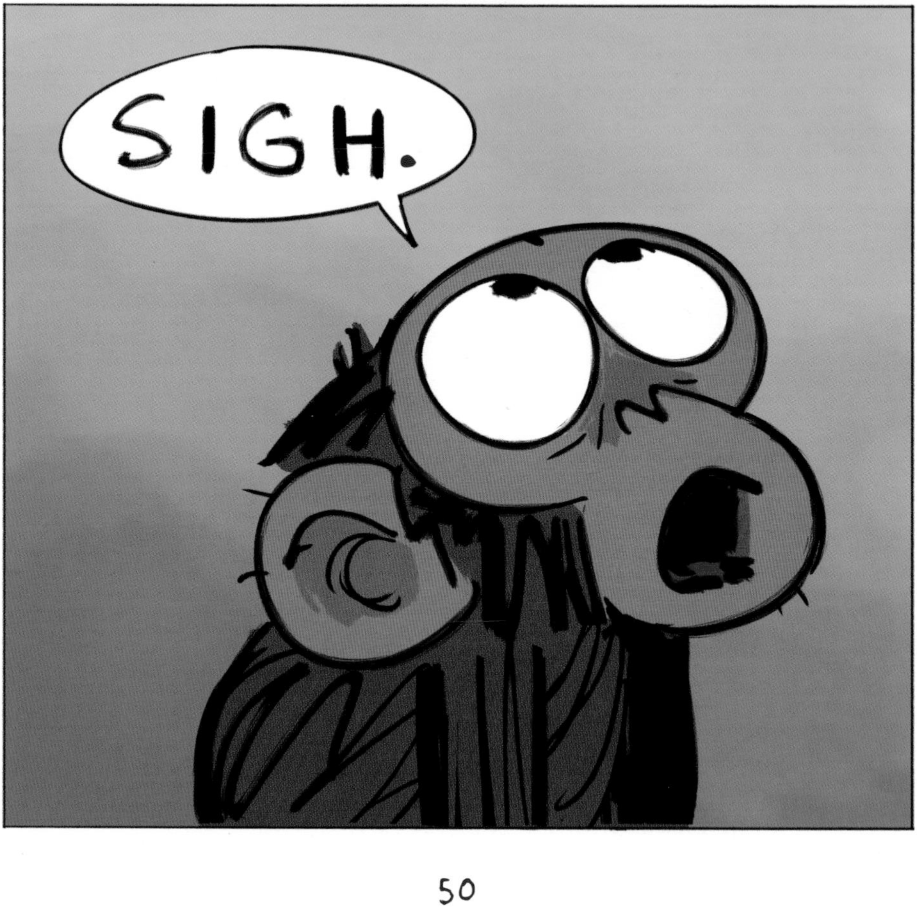
SIGH.

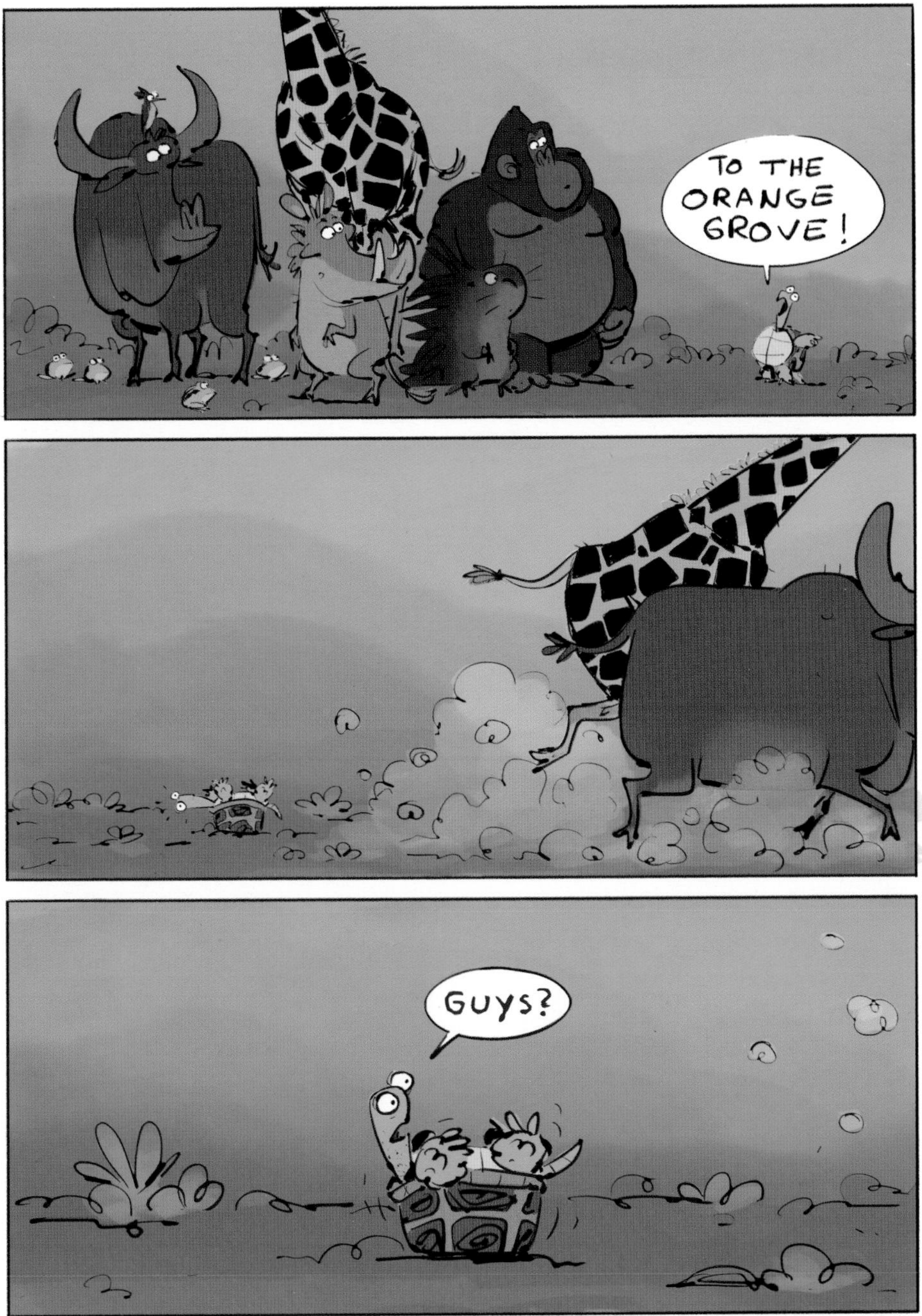
TO THE ORANGE GROVE!
GUYS?

TO BE CONTINUED

CHOMP & CHAT WITH CHIP PANZEE

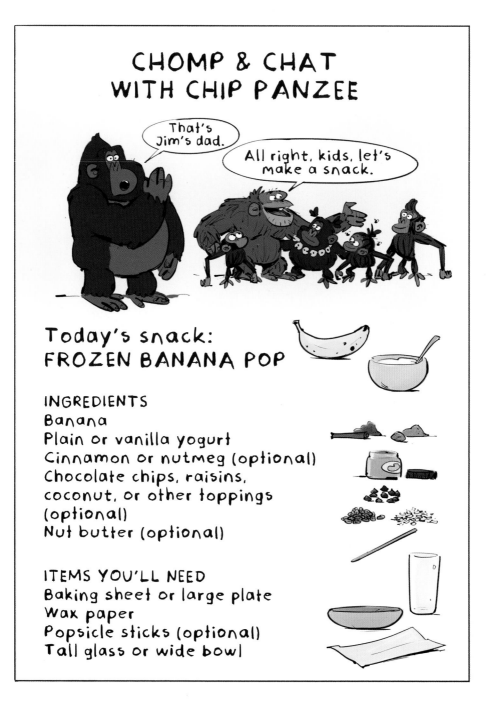

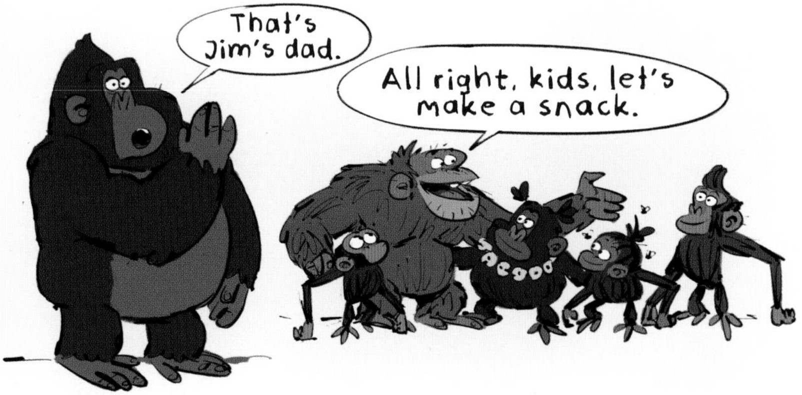
That's Jim's dad.
All right, kids, let's make a snack.

Today's snack: FROZEN BANANA POP

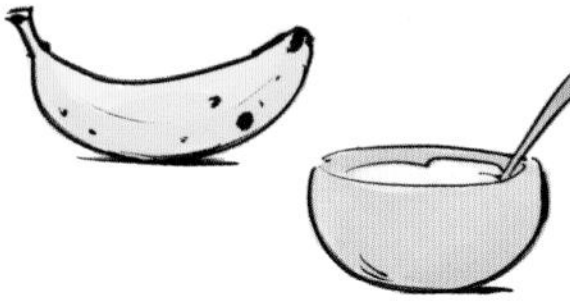

INGREDIENTS
Banana
Plain or vanilla yogurt
Cinnamon or nutmeg (optional)
Chocolate chips, raisins, coconut, or other toppings (optional)
Nut butter (optional)

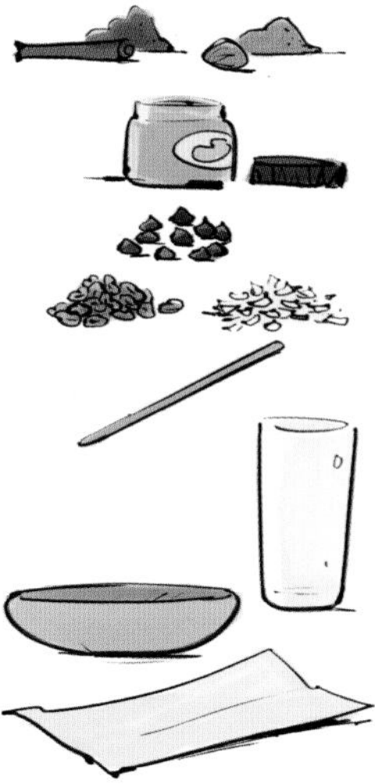

ITEMS YOU'LL NEED
Baking sheet or large plate
Wax paper
Popsicle sticks (optional)
Tall glass or wide bowl

INSTRUCTIONS

1. Put a banana-size piece of wax paper on a baking sheet or plate.

2. If you want to use a Popsicle stick, gently insert it into one end of a peeled banana.

3. Put the banana on the baking sheet or plate, and freeze for 30 minutes.

4. Put the yogurt into a tall glass or wide bowl. If you like cinnamon or nutmeg, mix a little in. Dip the banana into the yogurt.

5. Roll it in the topping(s) of your choice.

6. Freeze the banana for one hour.

7. If you like nut butter, you can use some as a dip or spread it on your banana.

8. Enjoy!

Like me. I'm a pop!

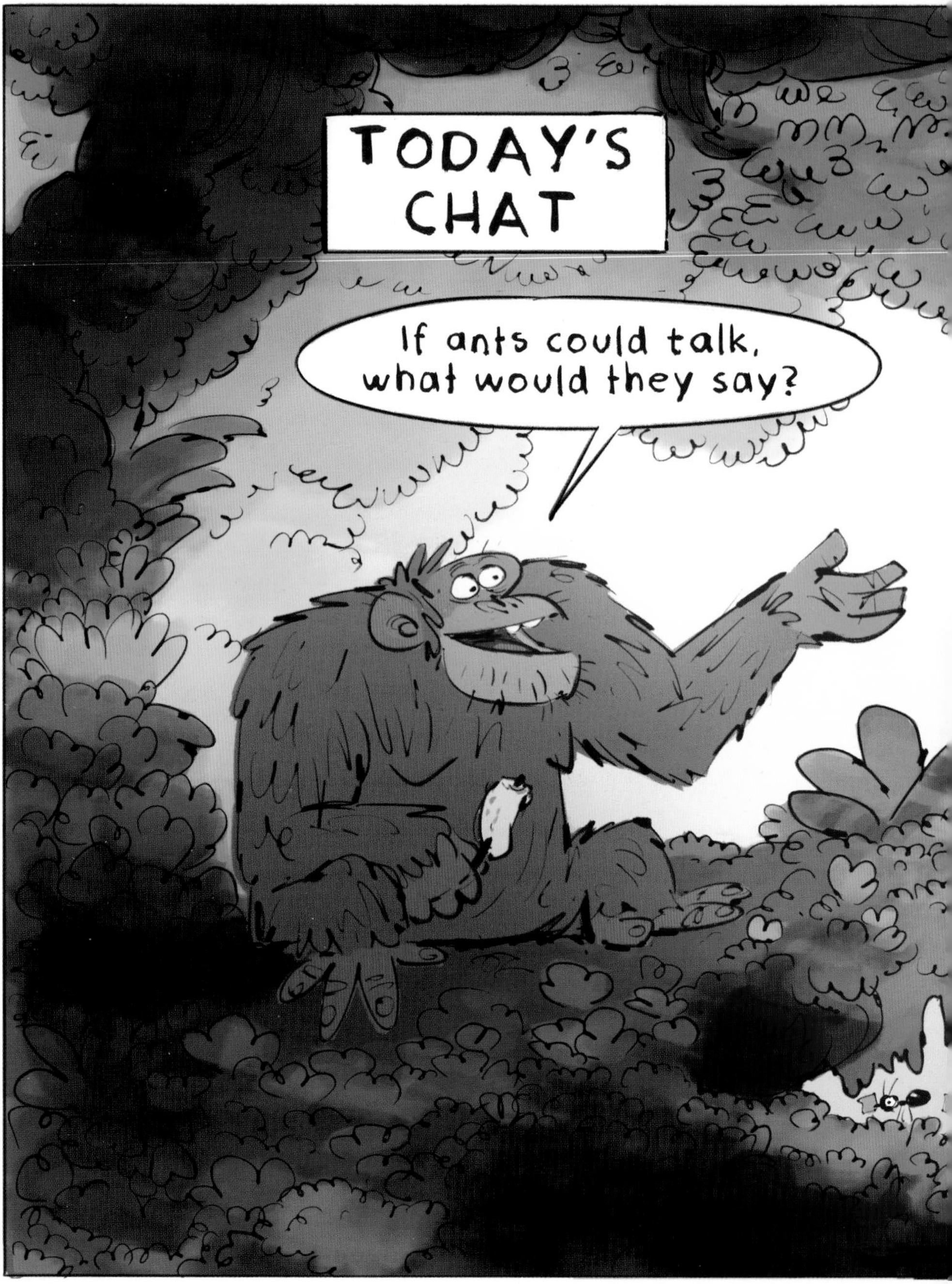
TODAY'S CHAT
If ants could talk, what would they say?

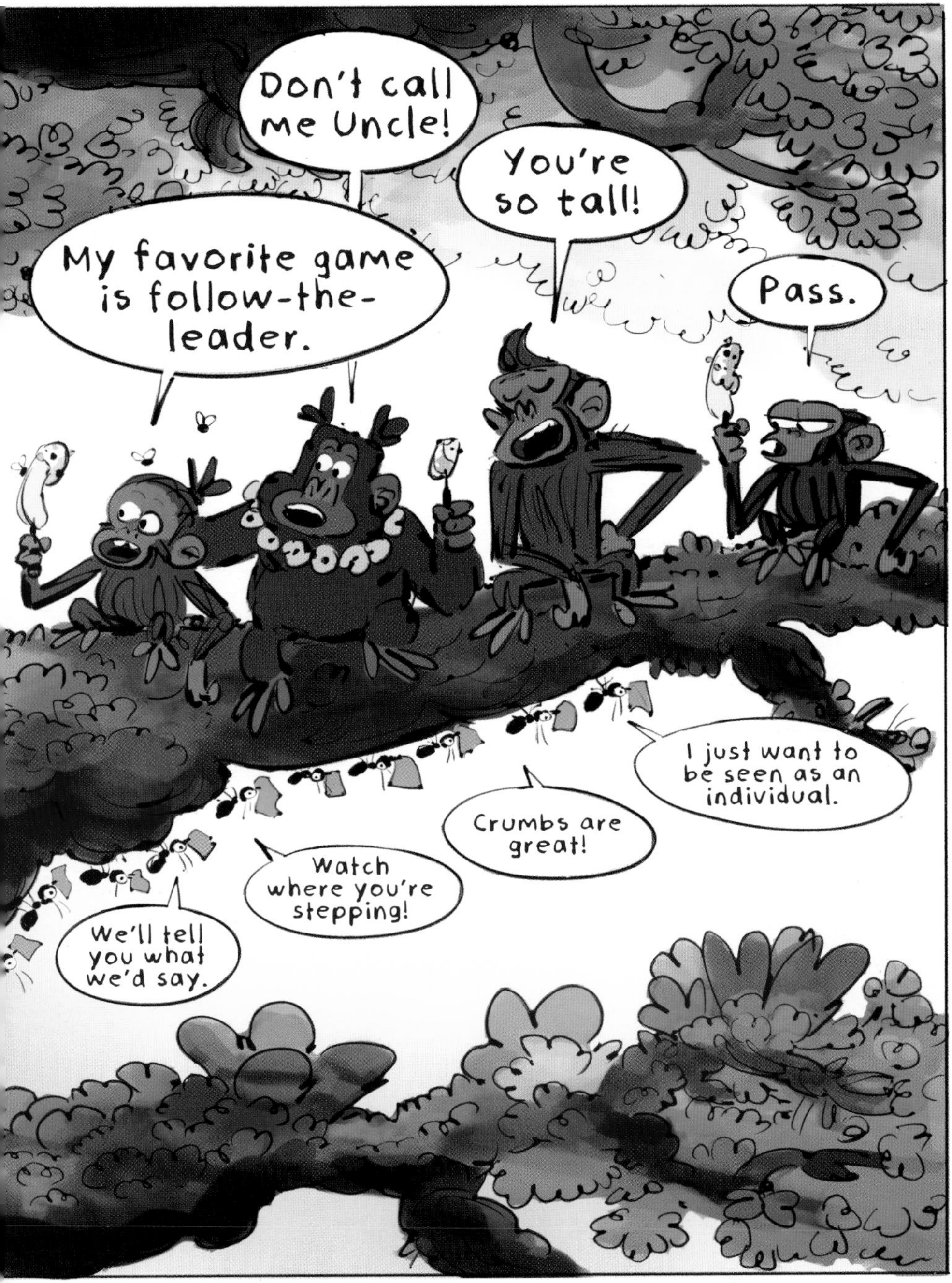
My favorite game is follow-the-leader.
Don't call me Uncle!
You're so tall!
Pass.
I just want to be seen as an individual.
Crumbs are great!
Watch where you're stepping!
We'll tell you what we'd say.

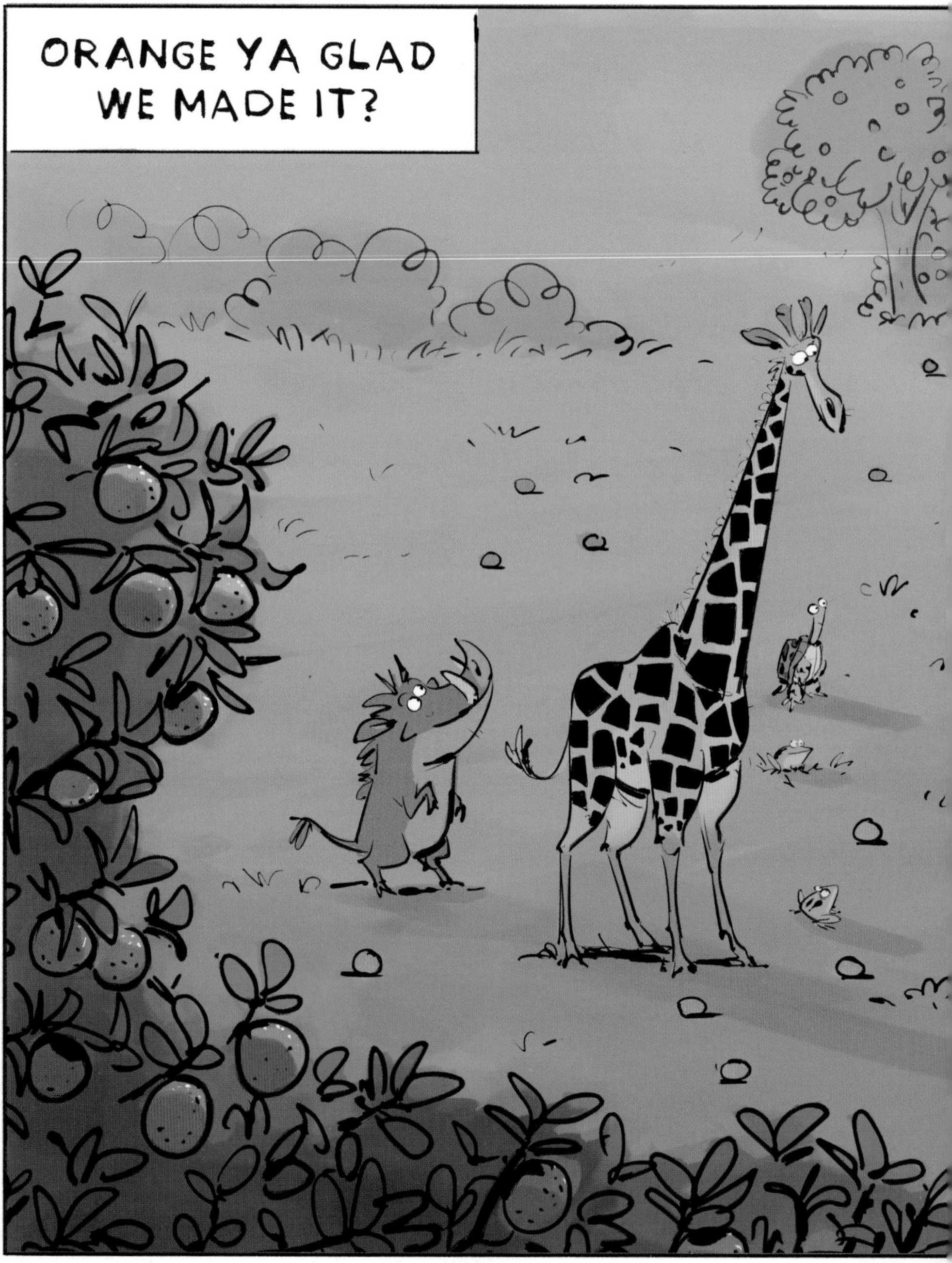
ORANGE YA GLAD WE MADE IT?

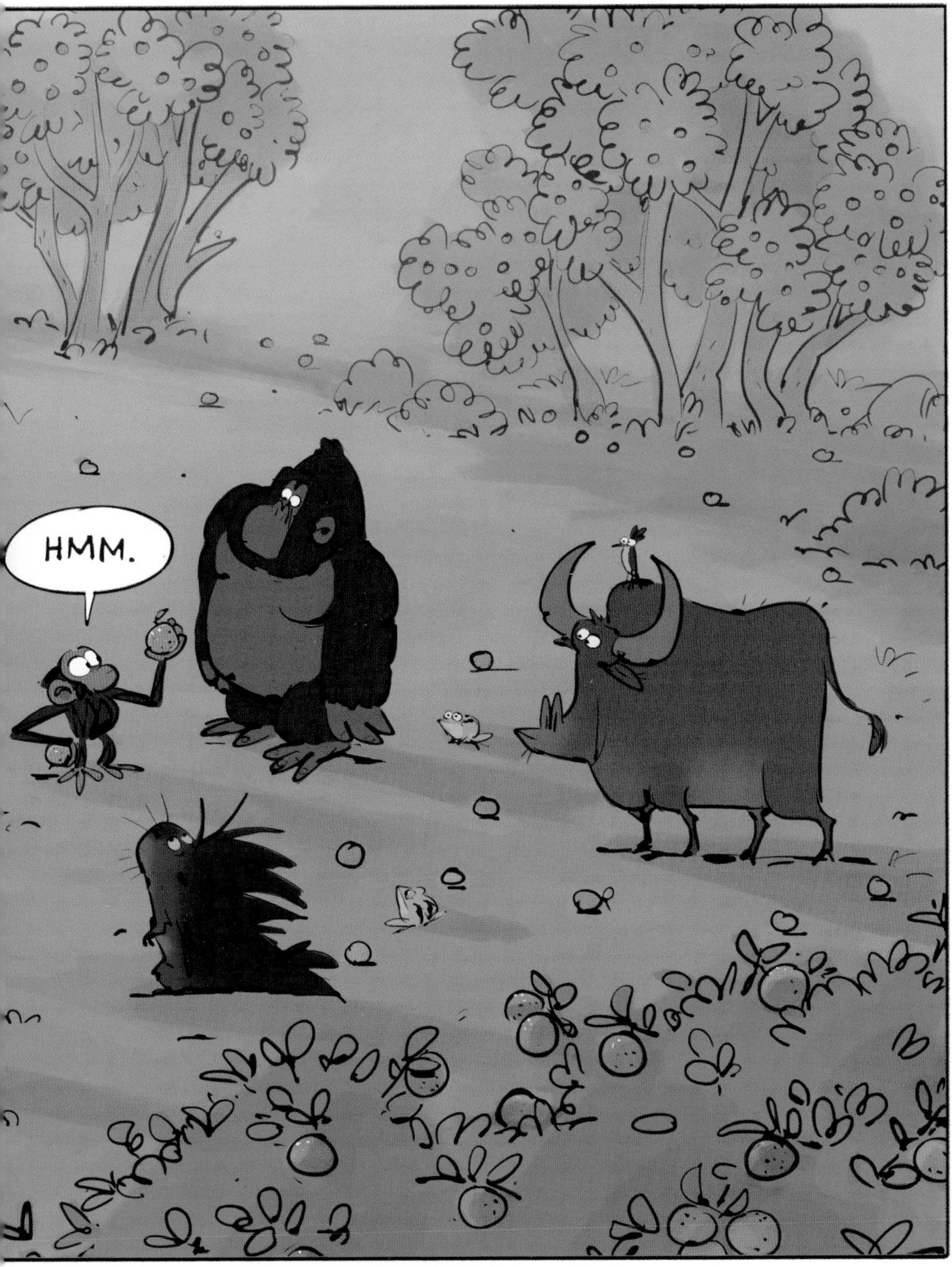
HMM.

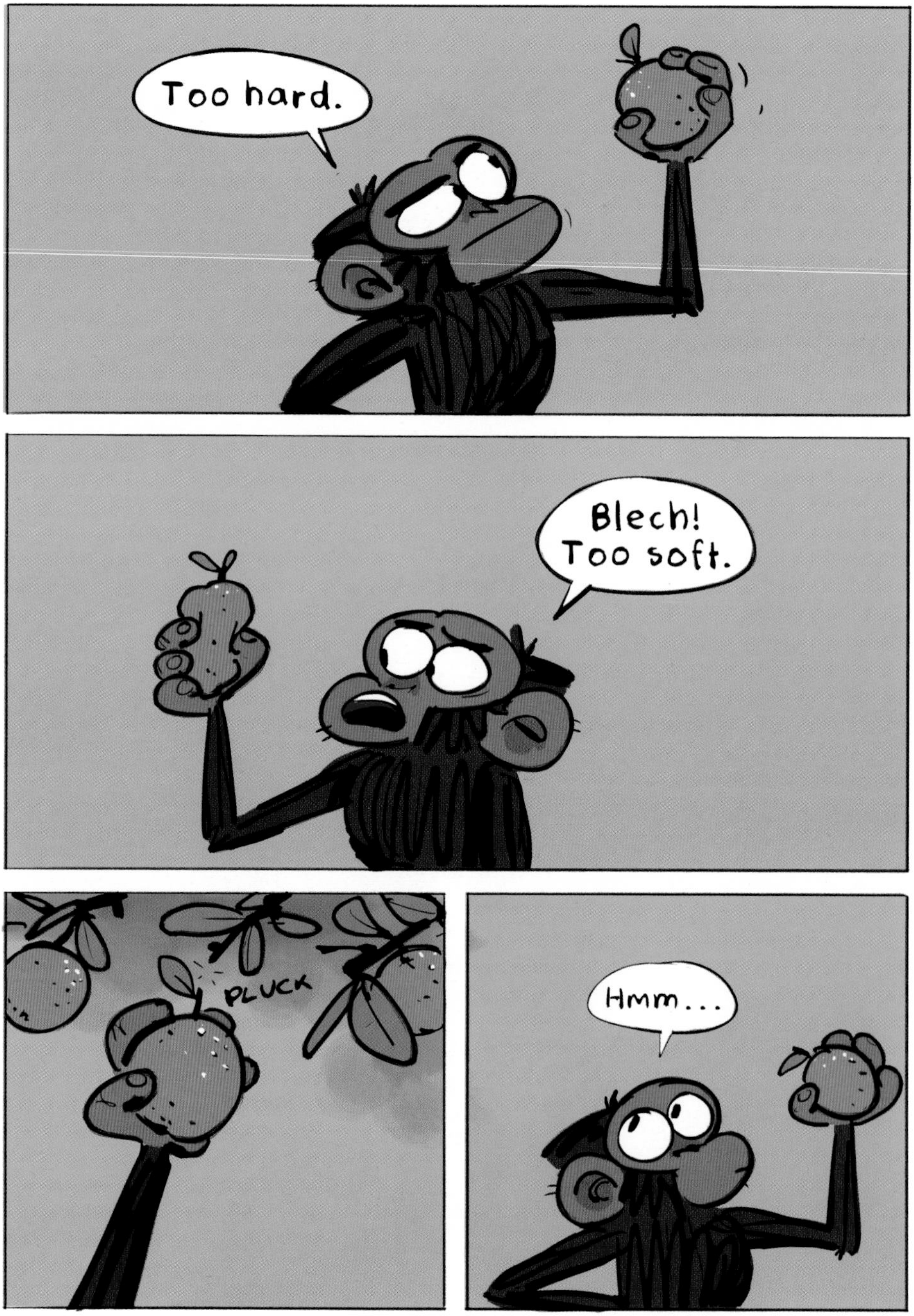
Too hard.
Blech! Too soft.
PLUCK
Hmm...

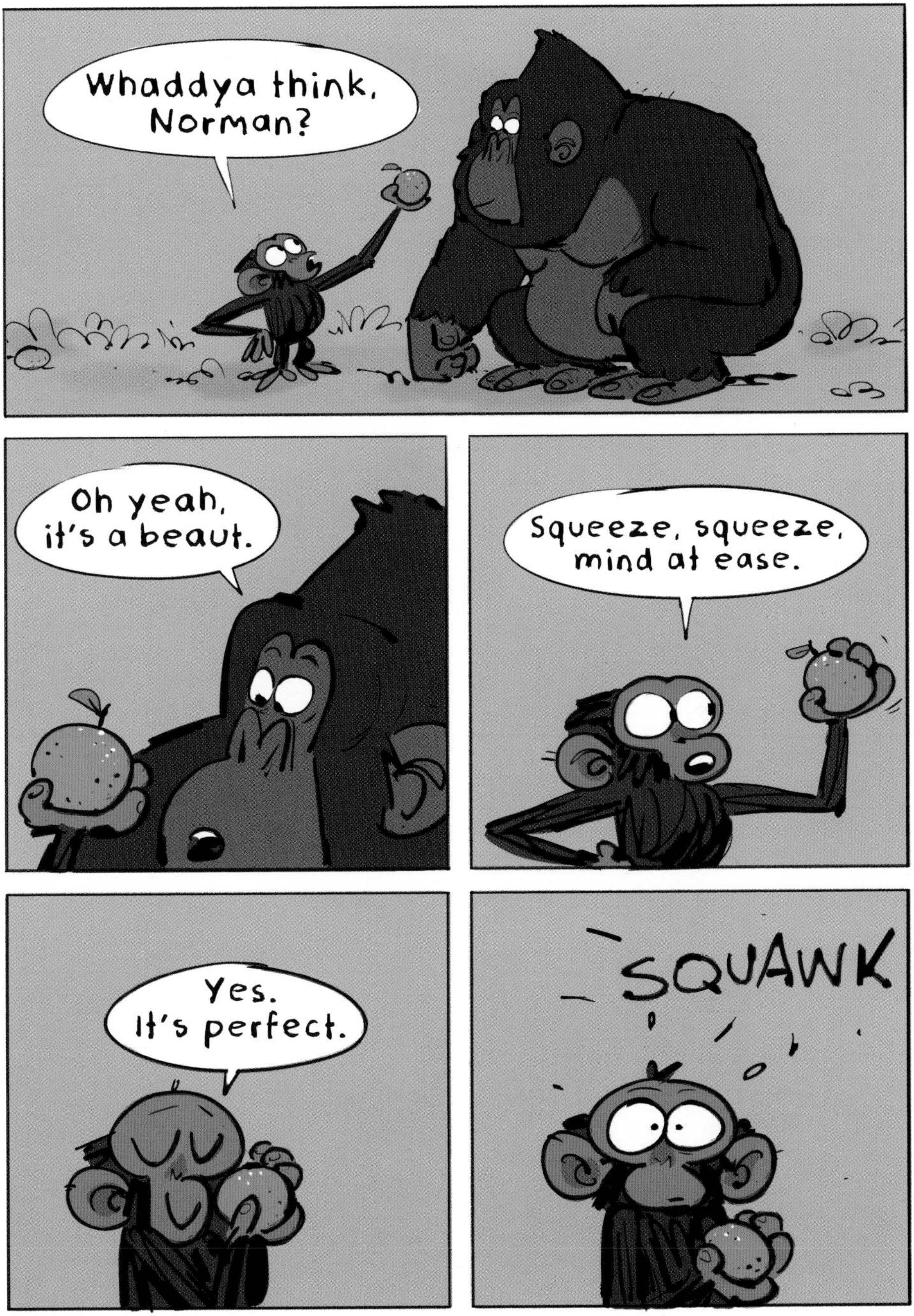
Whaddya think, Norman?
Oh yeah, it's a beaut.
Squeeze, squeeze, mind at ease.
Yes. It's perfect.
SQUAWK

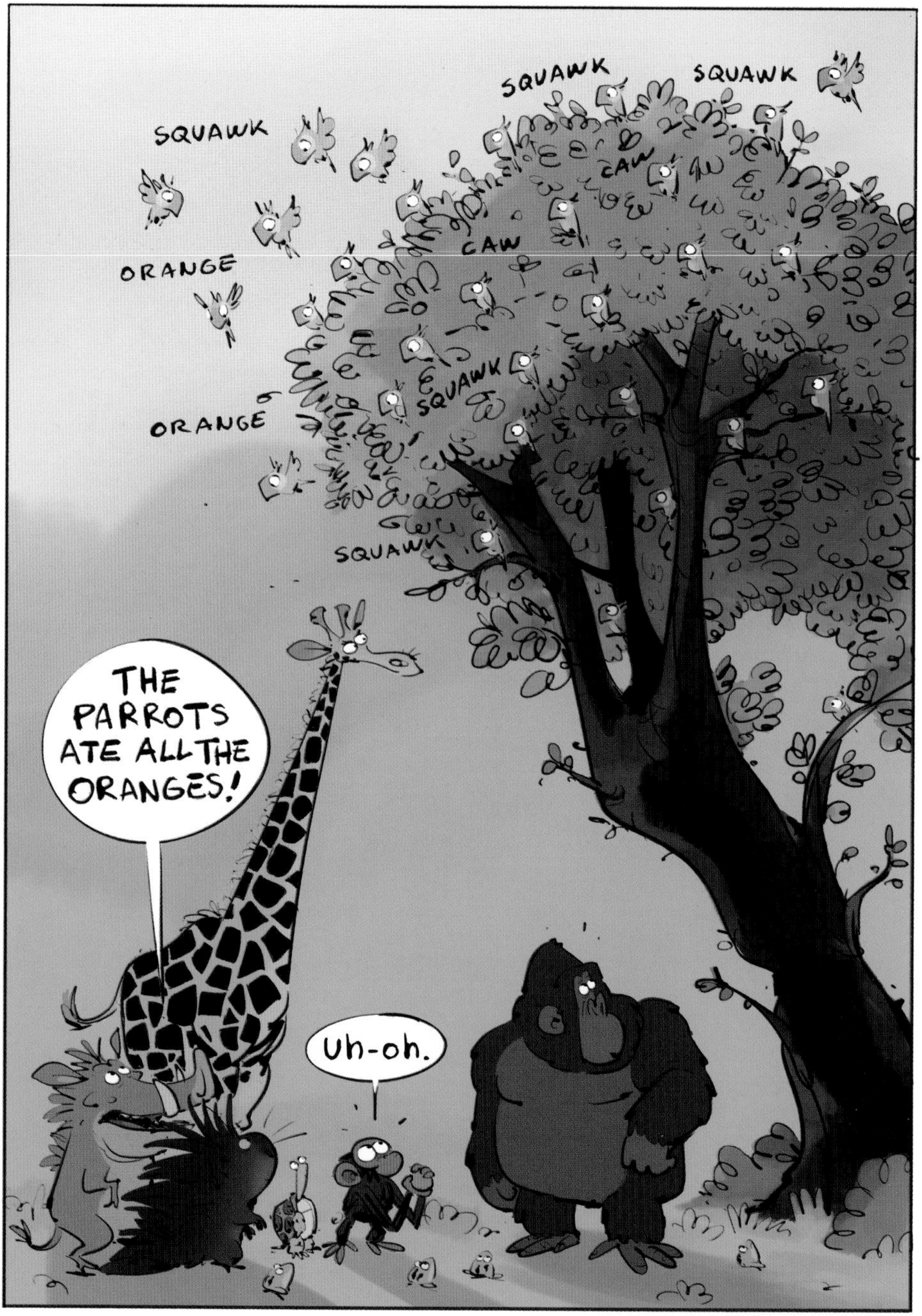
SQUAWK
SQUAWK
SQUAWK
ORANGE
CAW
CAW
ORANGE
SQUAWK
SQUAWK
THE PARROTS ATE ALL THE ORANGES!
Uh-oh.

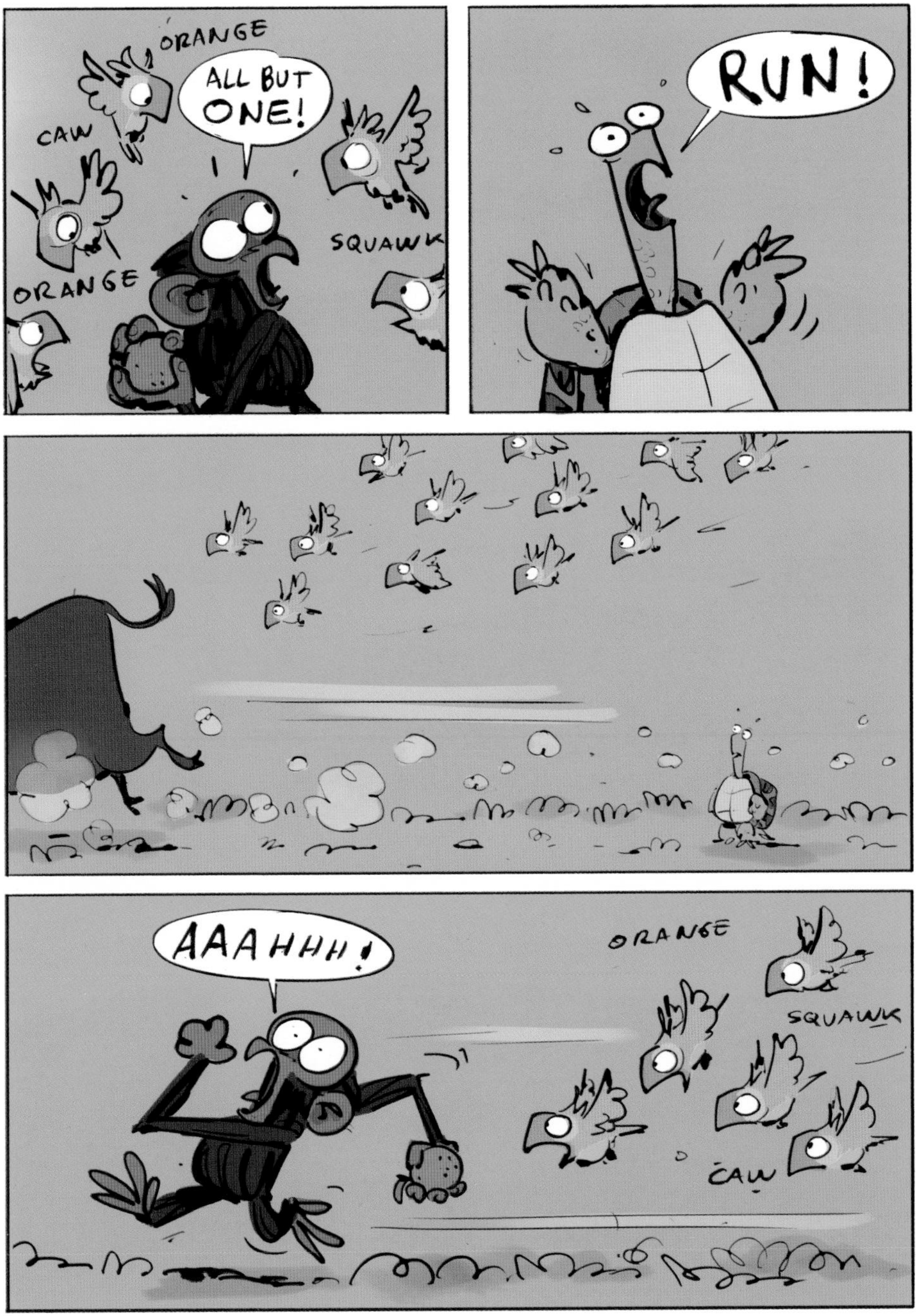
ORANGE
CAW
ALL BUT ONE!
SQUAWK
ORANGE
RUN!
AAAHHH!
ORANGE
SQUAWK
CAW

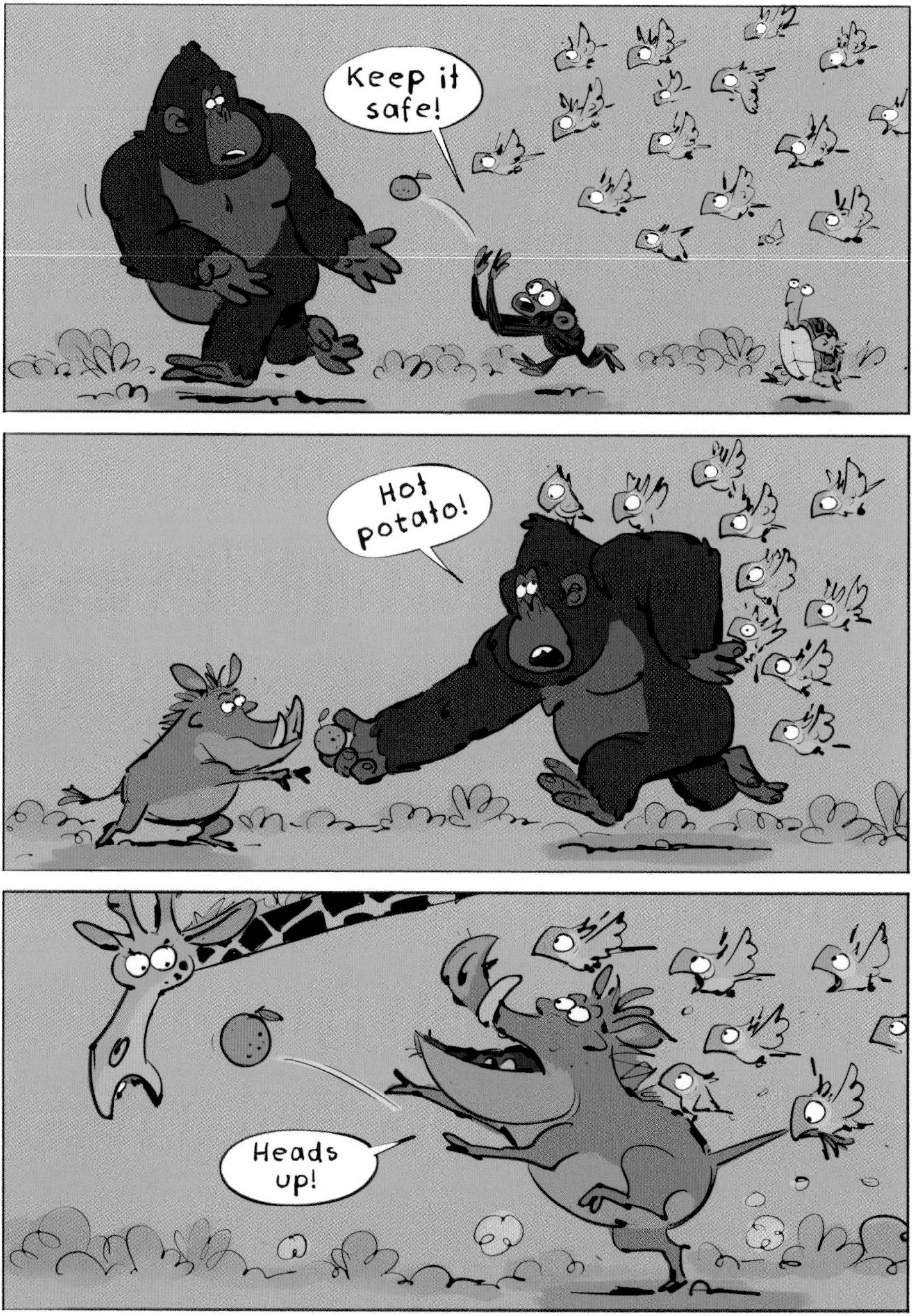
Keep it safe!
Hot potato!
Heads up!

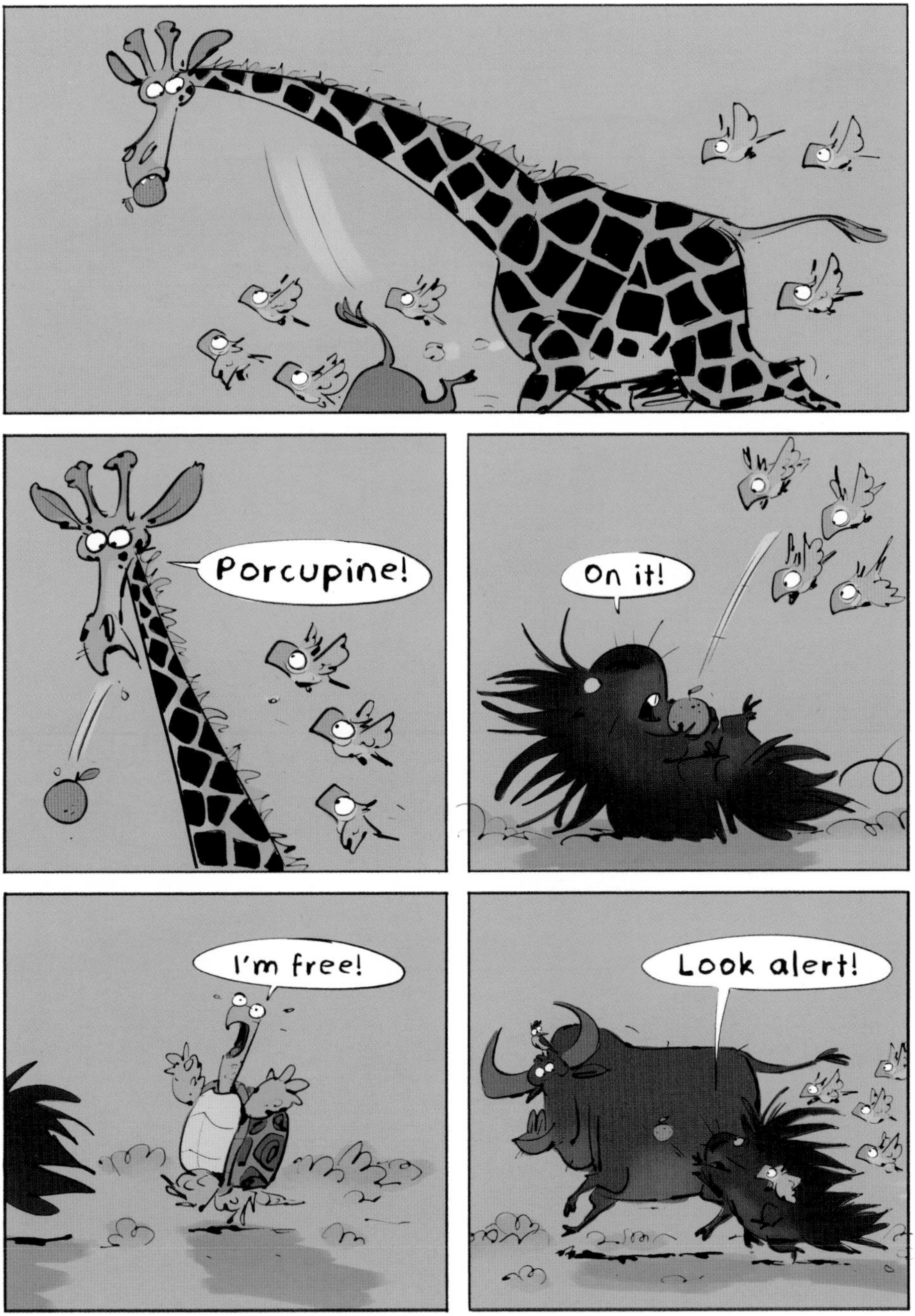

Porcupine!
On it!
I'm free!
Look alert!

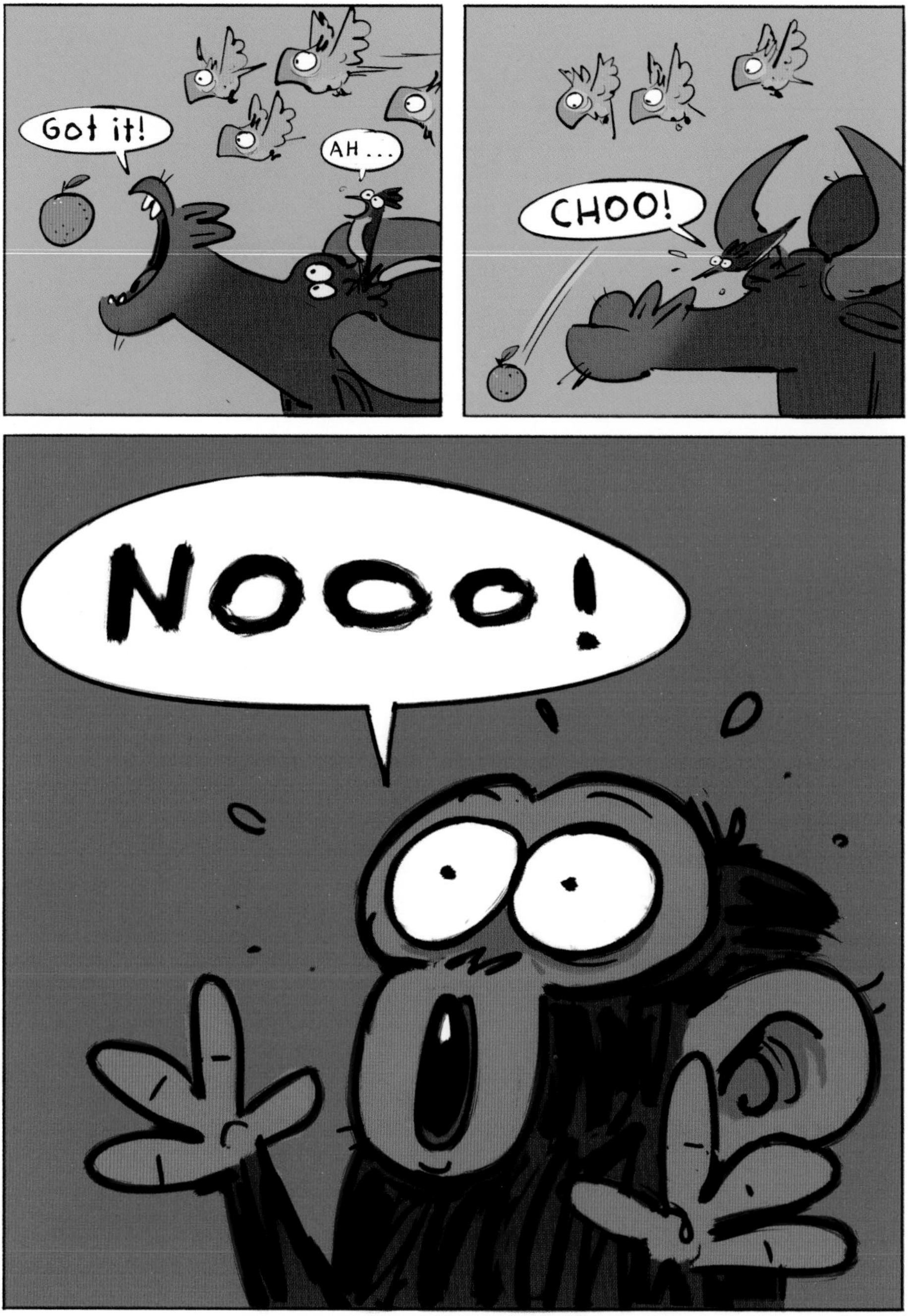
Got it!
AH...
CHOO!
NOOO!

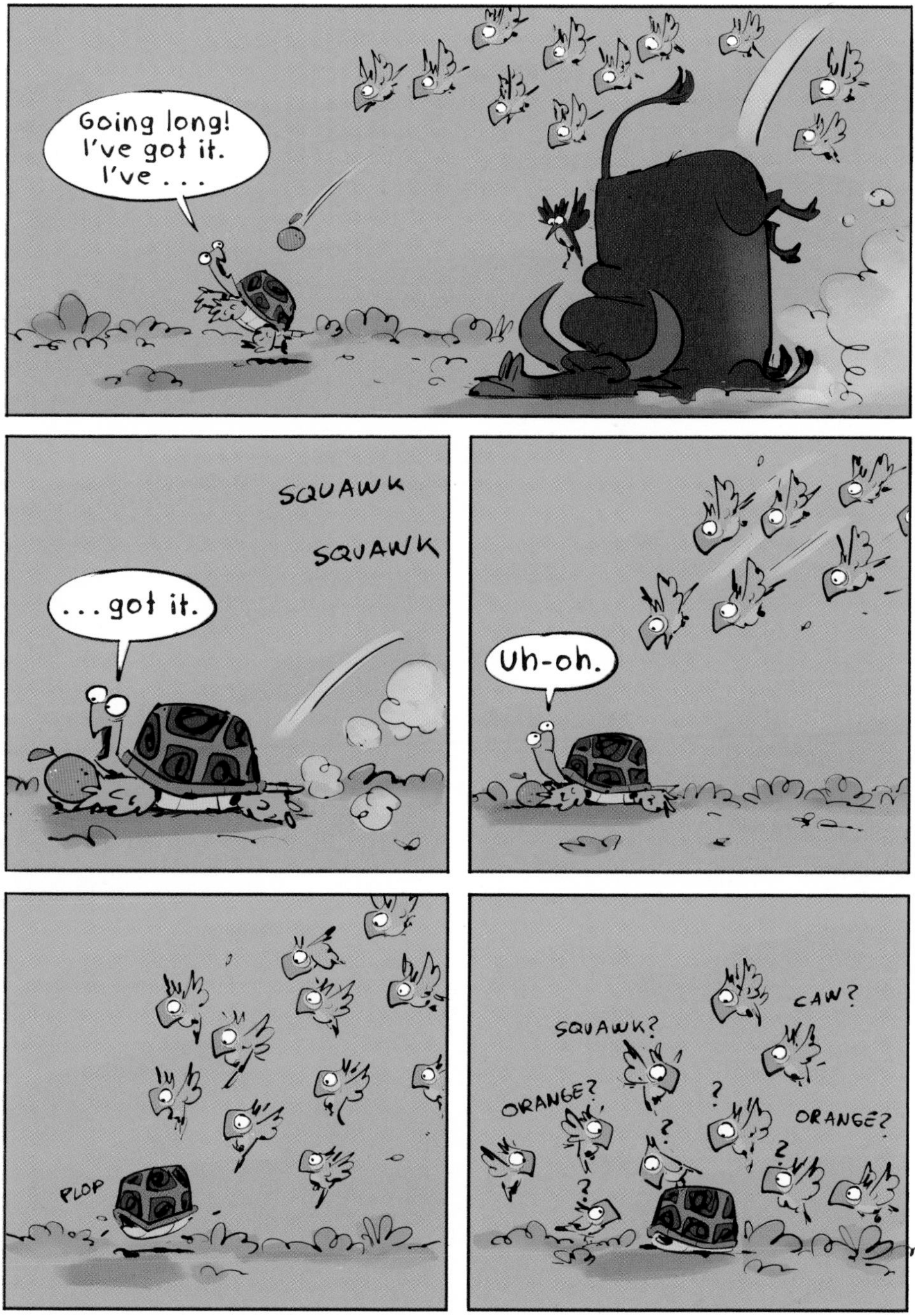
Going long! I've got it. I've . . .
SQUAWK
SQUAWK
. . . got it.
Uh-oh.
PLOP
SQUAWK?
CAW?
ORANGE?
ORANGE?

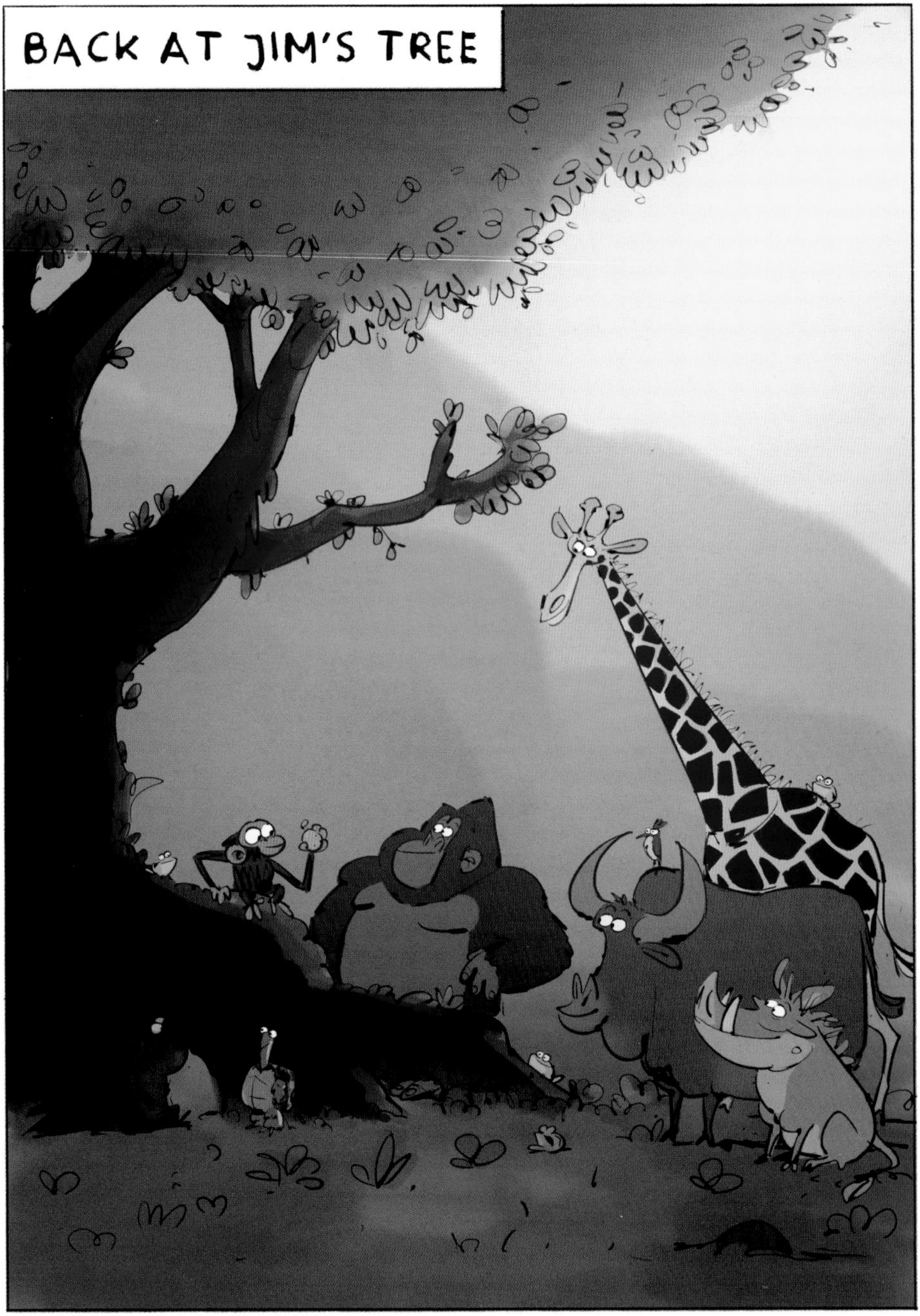
BACK AT JIM'S TREE

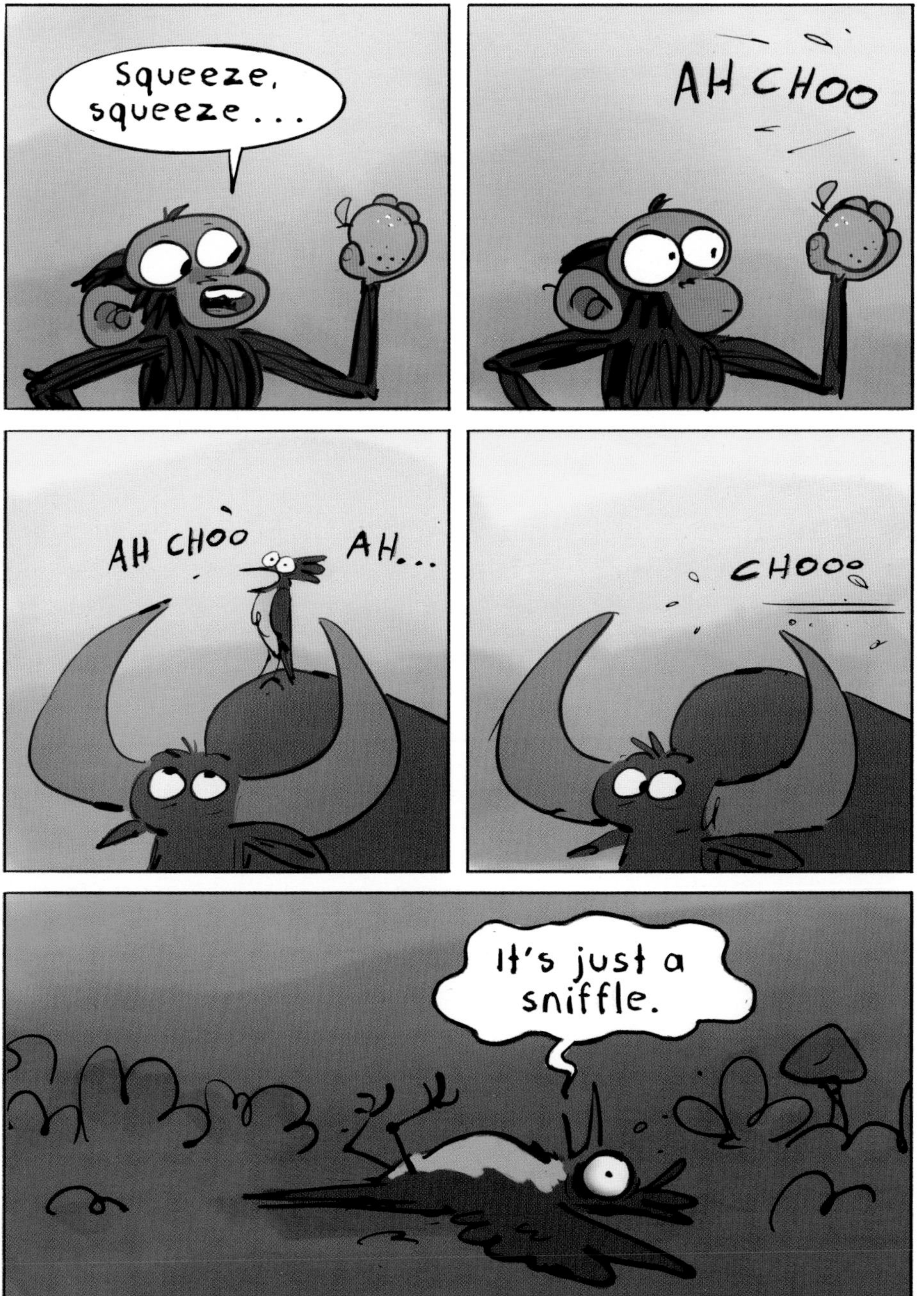

Squeeze, squeeze . . .
AH CHOO
AH CHOO
AH. . .
CHOOO
It's just a sniffle.

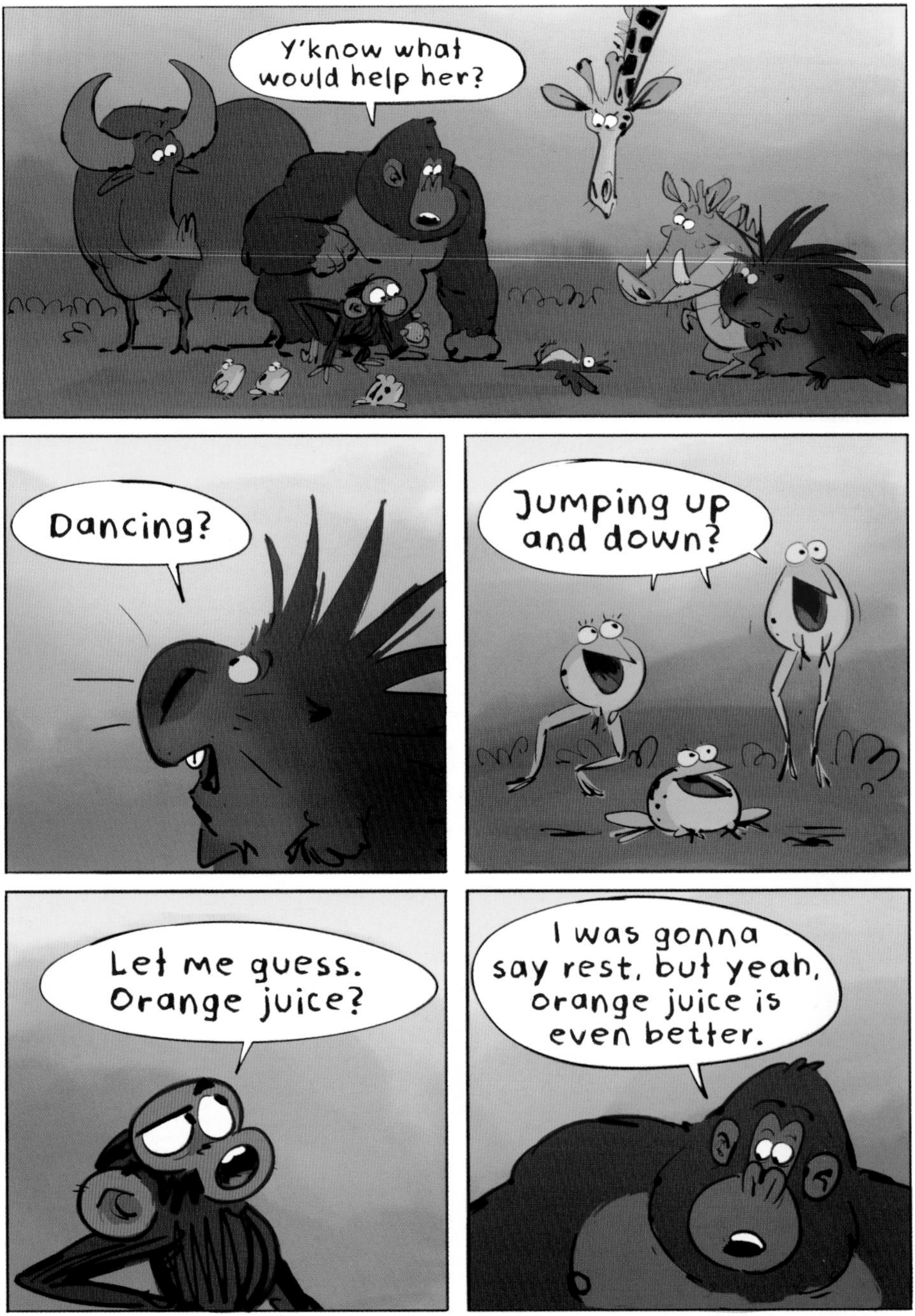
Y'know what would help her?
Dancing?
Jumping up and down?
Let me guess. Orange juice?
I was gonna say rest, but yeah, orange juice is even better.

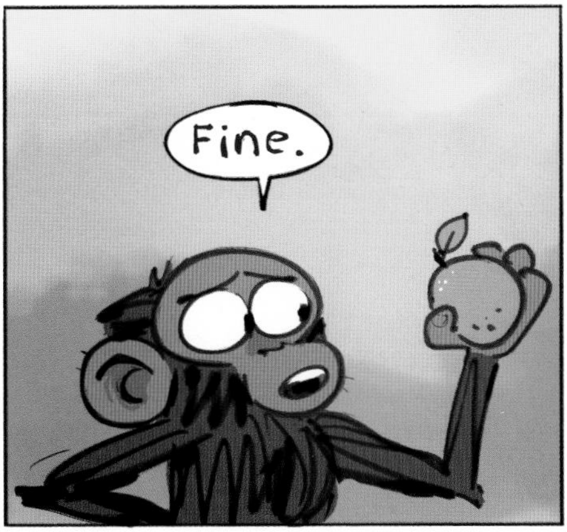
Fine.

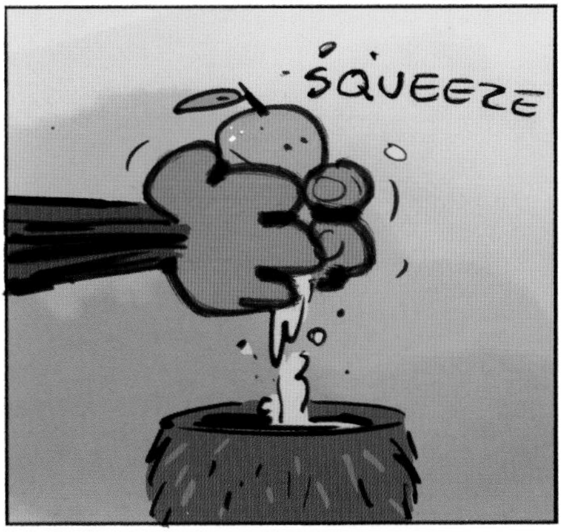
SQUEEZE

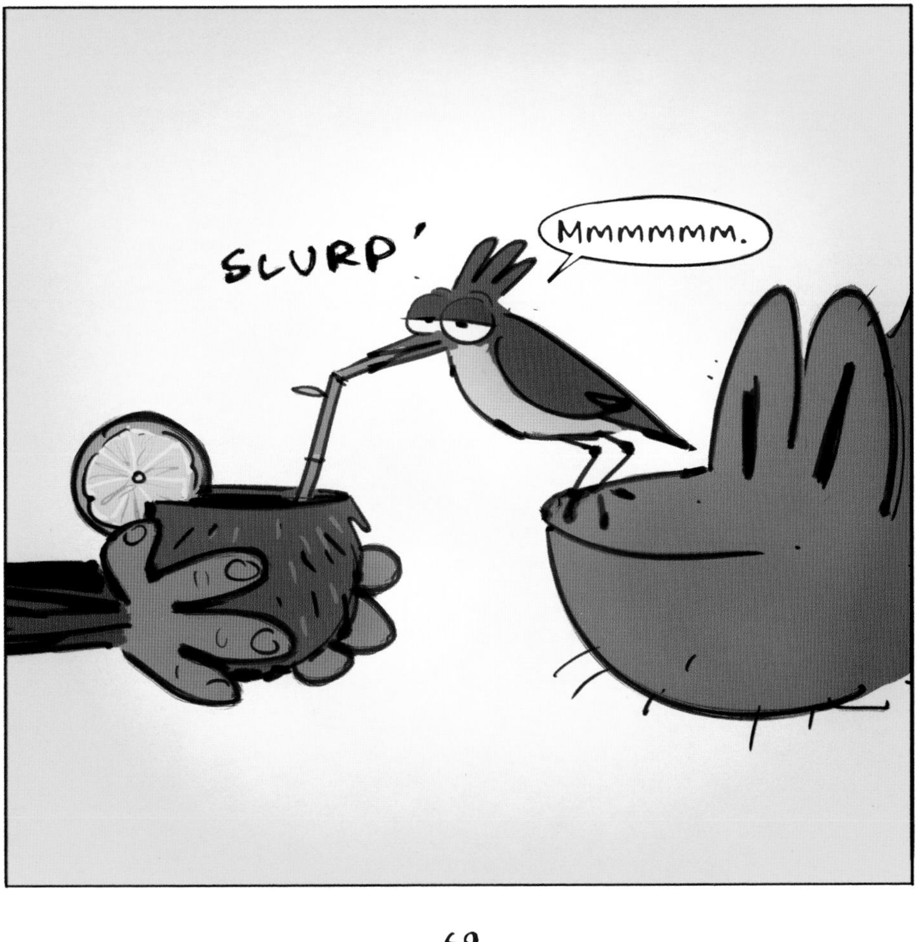
SLURP
Mmmmmm.

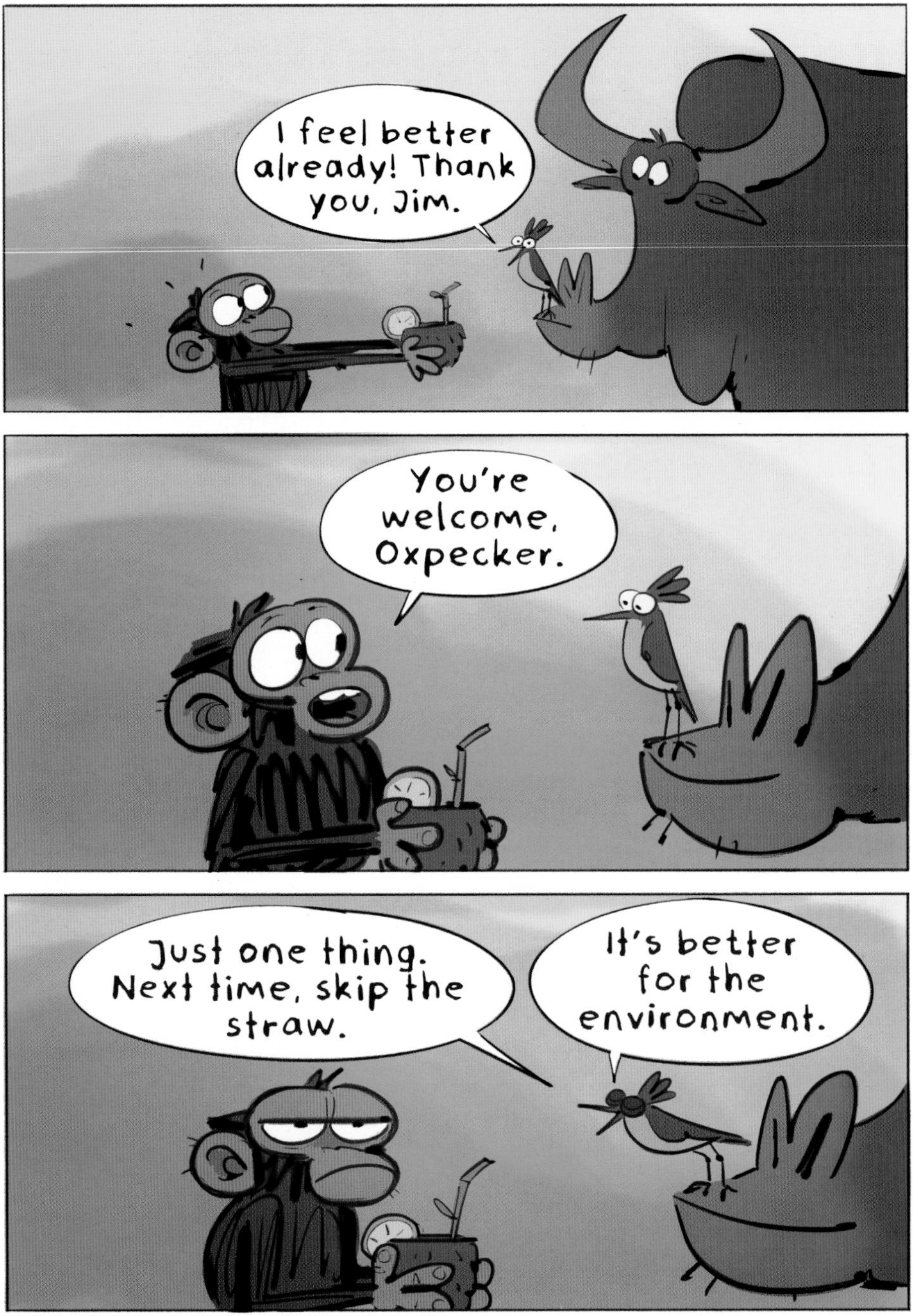
I feel better already! Thank you, Jim.
You're welcome, Oxpecker.
Just one thing. Next time, skip the straw.
It's better for the environment.

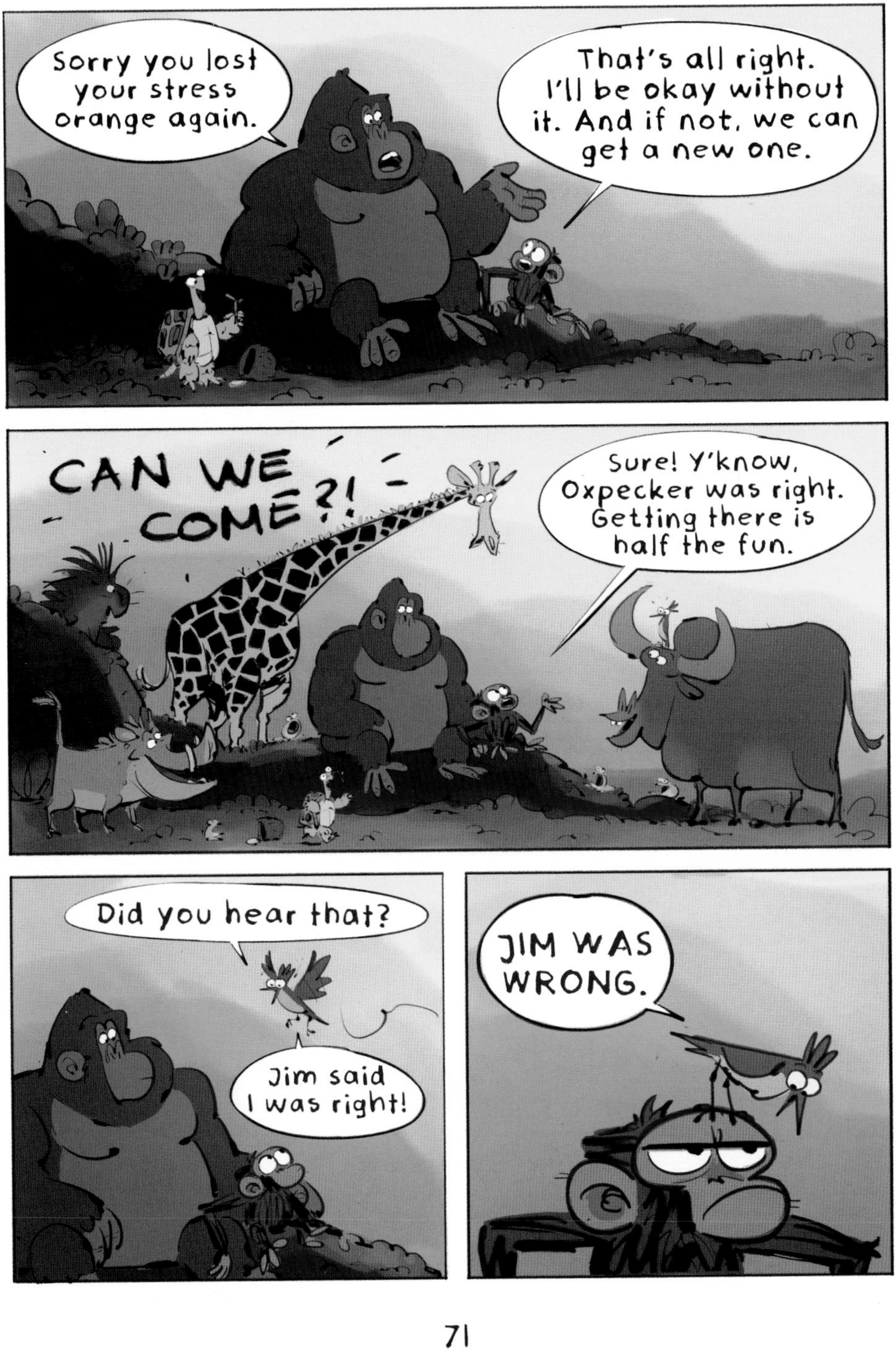
Sorry you lost your stress orange again.
That's all right. I'll be okay without it. And if not, we can get a new one.
CAN WE COME?!
Sure! Y'know, Oxpecker was right. Getting there is half the fun.
Did you hear that?
Jim said I was right!
JIM WAS WRONG.

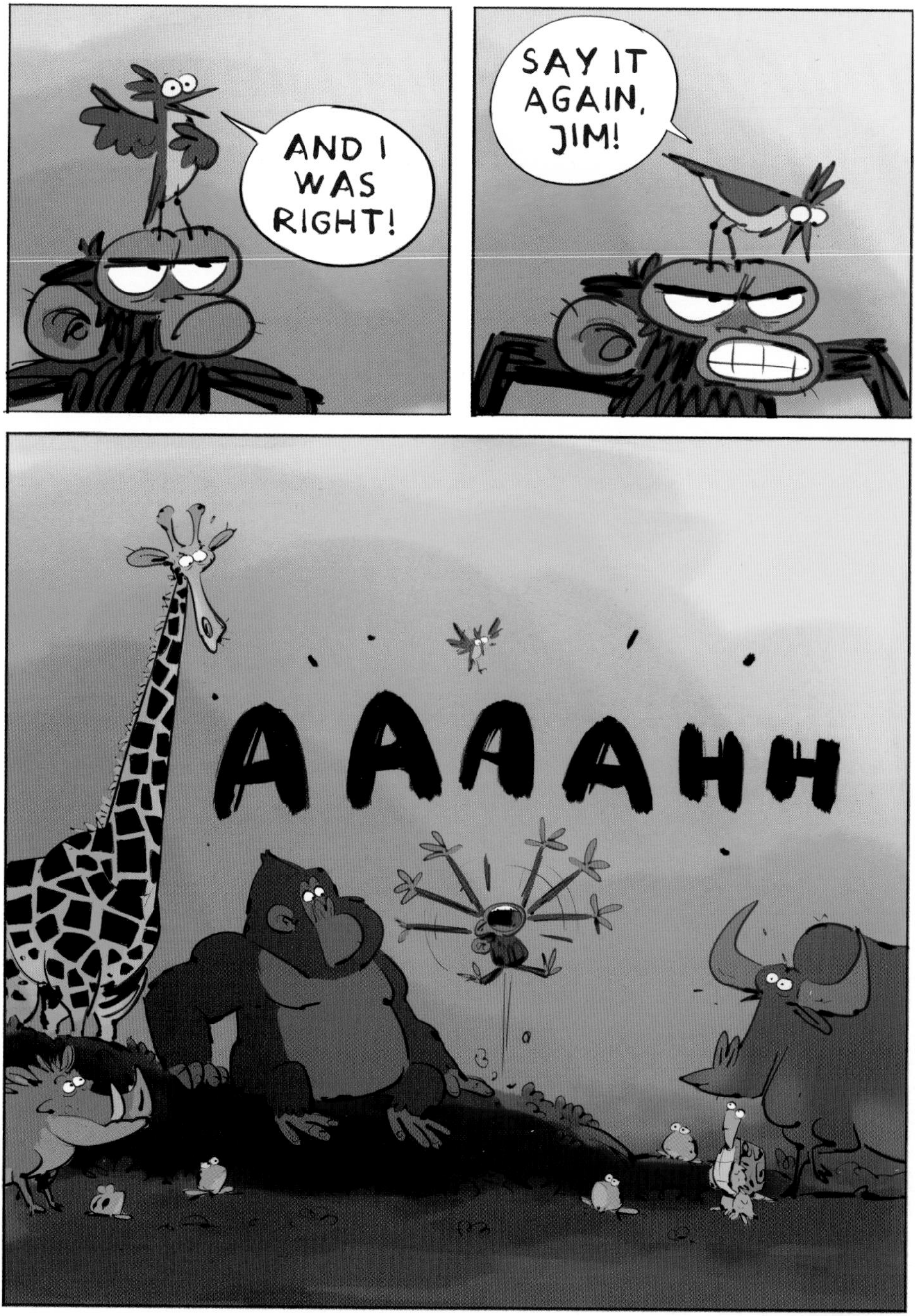
AND I WAS RIGHT!
SAY IT AGAIN, JIM!
AAAAHH

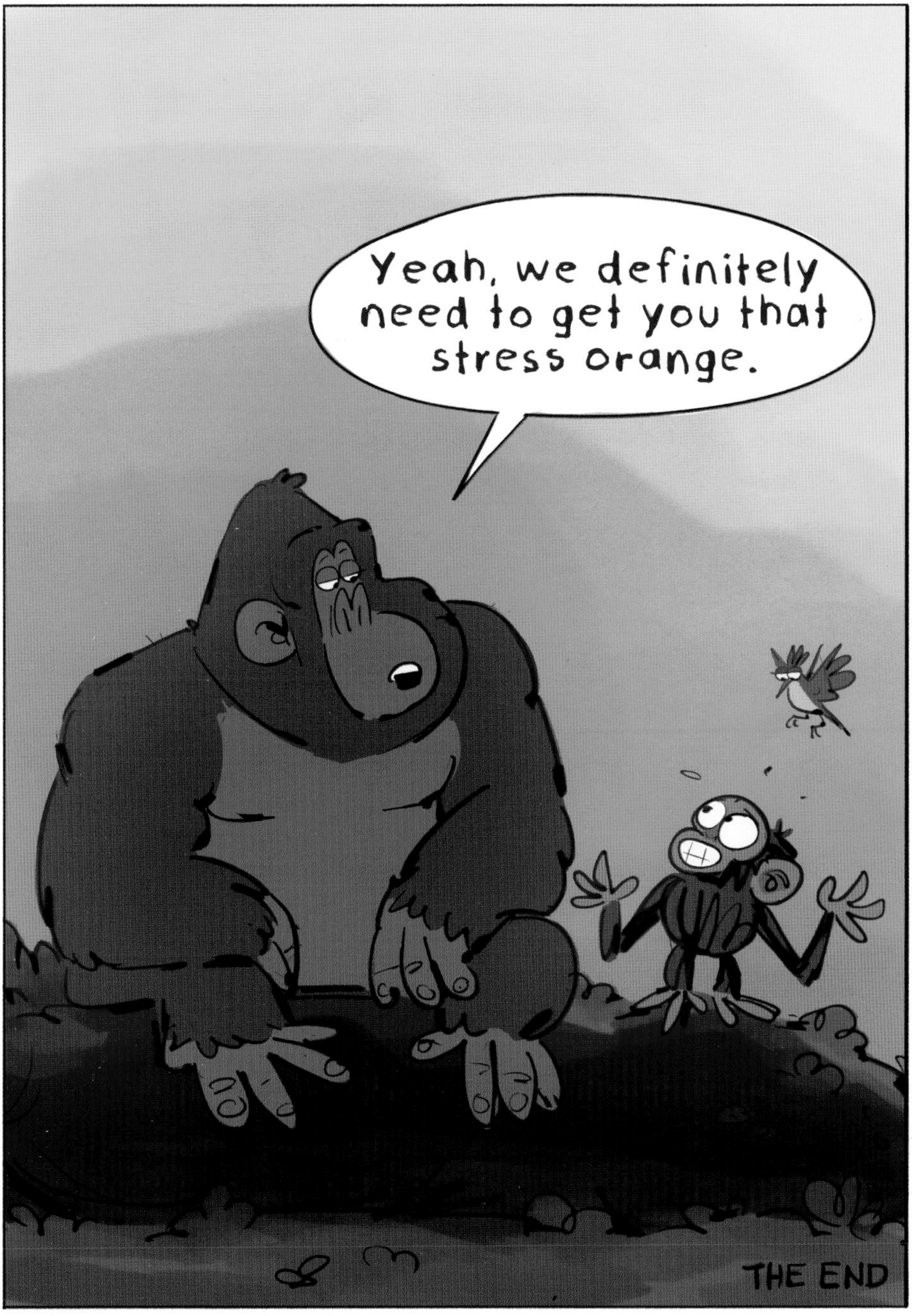
Yeah, we definitely need to get you that stress orange.
THE END

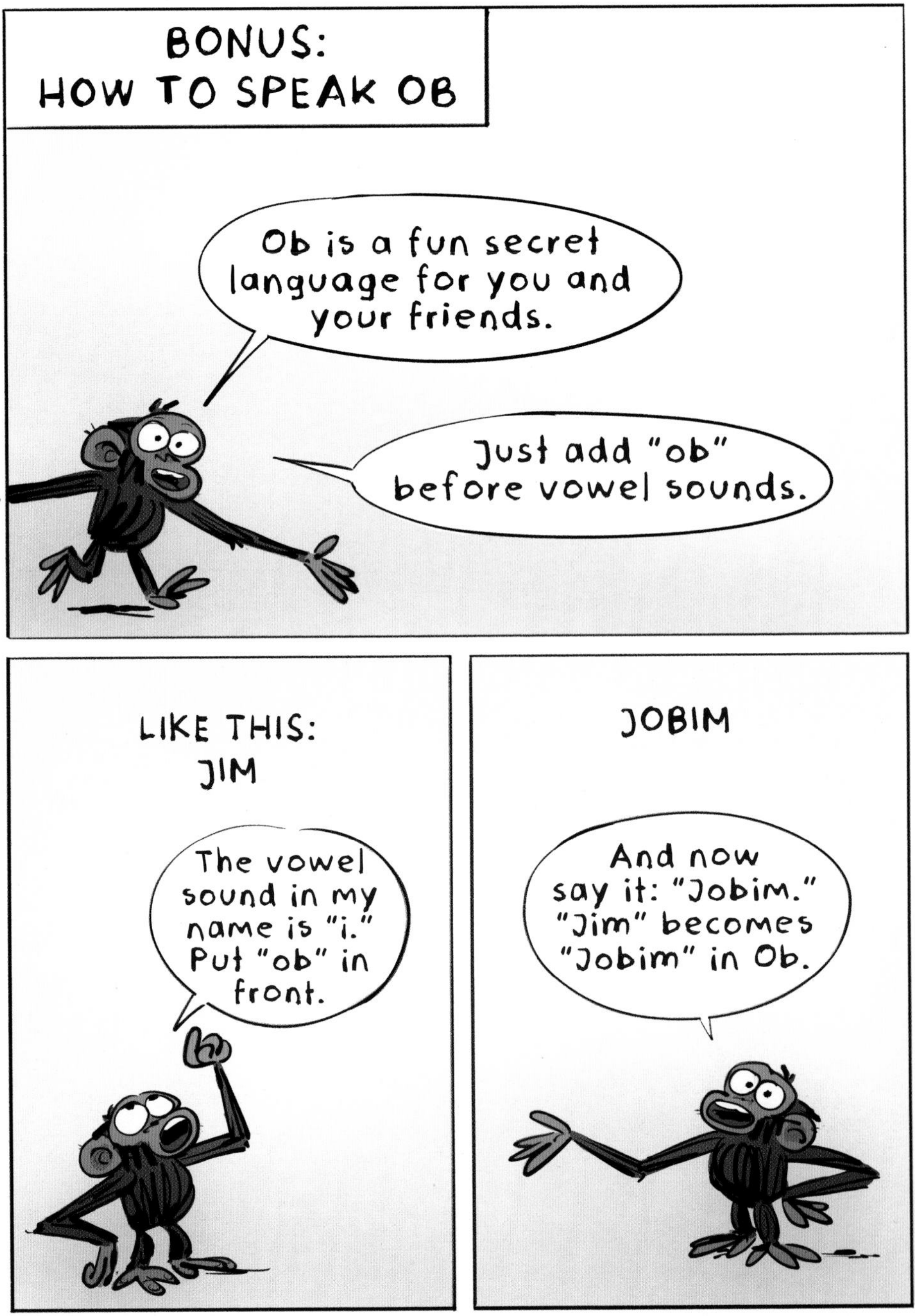
BONUS:
HOW TO SPEAK OB
Ob is a fun secret language for you and your friends.
Just add "ob" before vowel sounds.
LIKE THIS:
JIM
The vowel sound in my name is "i." Put "ob" in front.
JOBIM
And now say it: "Jobim." "Jim" becomes "Jobim" in Ob.

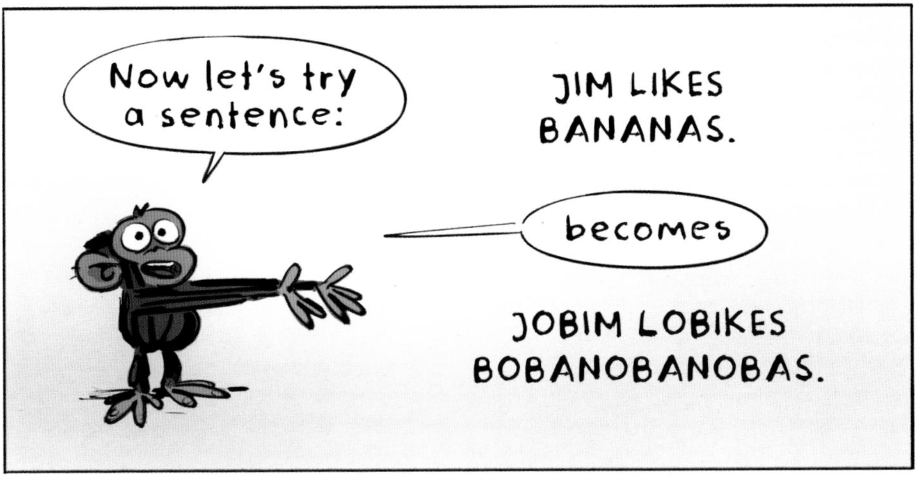
Now let's try a sentence:
JIM LIKES BANANAS.
becomes
JOBIM LOBIKES BOBANOBANOBAS.

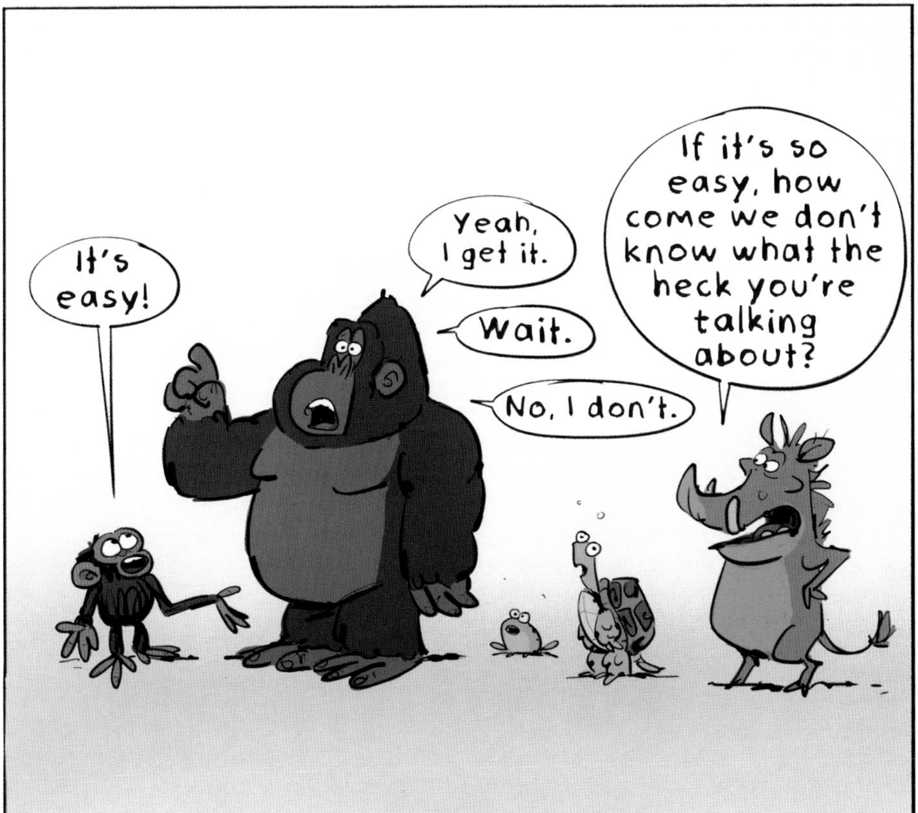
It's easy!
Yeah, I get it.
Wait.
No, I don't.
If it's so easy, how come we don't know what the heck you're talking about?

Suzanne Lang takes a walk every Wednesday morning. She loves it when she sees bunnies, deer, ducks, and squirrels on her walk, but she doesn't like it so much when other humans ask to join her. After her walk, Suzanne likes to go home and write. Sometimes she writes scripts for cartoons, and sometimes she writes books. You may have read some of the other Grumpy Monkey books she wrote. Suzanne loves secret languages and has been fluent in Ob since she was fourteen.

Max Lang drew every single picture in this book. If you go back and try to count them, you will realize that is a lot of drawings! Max has always liked drawing a lot. Other things he likes a lot are making animated movies (one movie he made is called *The Gruffalo*, and another is called *Room on the Broom*), making books, and eating apples. In fact, he likes eating apples so much that he eats them right down to the core until there is almost nothing left but the stem and seeds. It drives his wife crazy.